CHEECHAKO

Jonathan Thomas Stratman

FOR
MY MOTHER,
ETHEL STRATMAN

Each night after supper she read to my brothers and me as we did the dishes. It was the only way she could keep us from attacking each other. *Out of the Silent Planet*, *Wind in the Willows*, *The Old Curiosity Shop*, *Sherlock Holmes*, all of the Narnia books, and many more. And that's how it all started.

ACKNOWLEDGMENTS

Versions of some chapters originally appeared in
CRICKET, the children's magazine.

Cover art:
Jesse JoshuaWatson, Illustrator
www.jessewatson.com
.

CHAPTER 1

Will nearly made it to safety before they spotted him.

"Get him!" someone shouted. Will started running through the wet snow, bulky math book tucked under his elbow like a football. Gallumping along in his heavy wool jacket and knee-high rubber boots, he struggled for speed. His lungs burned as, panting and scrabbling for footing in the slush, he made for the safety of the school door.

Five boys chased Will, with Edwin in the lead. For no reason that Will could figure, Edwin and his friends had decided to make his life miserable by ambushing him before school, after school, or any other time it pleased them.

An ice ball slammed him on the ear, knocking the wool hat off his head, stinging as badly as a punch.

That's when they caught up and surrounded him. Edwin pushed through the others and jammed his face so close that Will smelled his breakfast breath.

"Leave me alone," gasped Will.

"Leave him alone," Edwin parroted, and turned to share a laugh with the other boys.

"You want to fight me now, Cheechako? Or are you chicken?" He turned to his friends. "I think he's chicken."

The clanging school bell signaled the end of Edwin's performance, but before Will could breathe a sigh of relief, Edwin shoved him backwards. Will's feet, on sheet ice skimmed with melt-water, shot out from under him. He went down hard, ice water soaking through jeans and boxers. Climbing to his feet, still clutching his book and grabbing his hat, Will turned and started up the concrete steps.

For the umpteenth time this winter, he read the painted sign above the door: Nenana Public School.

"Welcome to Alaska," he muttered to himself, his pants once again wet and cold and stuck to his butt.

Will had come out from Boston the summer before, reading *White Fang* and dreaming of adventures in the wilderness, of shooting a gun, tracking wolves, and mushing dogsleds.

So far, none of that had happened. He hadn't seen much wilderness, just this very drab little town. And since he hadn't managed to make a single friend, Will spent most of his afternoons lying on his bed, snacking, reading and missing his friends and his real life back in the States.

Now he found himself dreaming of Boston.

Still, he remembered that rush of excitement the day he arrived. Stepping down from the train, he made up his mind to explore. Not a big job as it turned out. Nenana, with its wide, dusty main street, stretched no more than four blocks in any direction from the old, wooden railroad depot.

This can't be all there is, he thought, his sneakers thumping hollowly on the board sidewalk. The town consisted of a ragged collection of mostly single-story, false-fronted buildings, their colors muted and dust coated to a uniform shade of washed-out gray.

Will counted a general store, hotel, post office, community center, four taverns, the Coffee Cup Café and the Pioneers of Alaska meeting hall where, his mother assured him, everybody went to the movie on Friday nights.

The town seemed oddly quiet. "Where are all the kids," Will asked his mother.

"In the fish camps."

"Fish camps? Summer camp for salmon?"

She smiled. "Clever, but you don't win the prize." She assumed her tour guide voice. "Indians on the Tanana River use a fish wheel—built of poles and chicken wire—that turns in the current and scoops up fish. Families who live in the fish camp, pitch in to clean and smoke the fish so they'll have enough food to last the winter."

It was Will's walking tour with his mother that first took him to the banks of the wide muddy river. It flowed swiftly, the surface writhing with whirlpools and rips. "Do people swim in this river," he asked.

"Not on purpose," his mother said. From where they stood they could see dockworkers, wearing bright orange life preservers, shifting cargo from railroad boxcars to large barges tied to flat-bottomed riverboats. "I've heard it's a tough river to get out of alive." She jabbed him playfully. "So no swimming!"

Will shuddered. "Not a chance." He looked around curiously at the bustling docks. "Where does all this stuff go?"

"Everywhere the river does. To villagers and miners and homesteaders—like we're going to be. Next summer we'll have our gear shipped out just like this."

Summer. Will sighed, suddenly back in his math class. He printed summer at the top of his math paper, then erased it. Would it ever be summer again? Snow arrived in October and now, in late May, had yet to completely melt.

Will sneaked a look at his classmates. Most of them were Athabascan Indians whom he didn't meet—or even see— until they returned from fish camp right before school started.

"Hey, Cheechako," someone had called to him on the first day. Will still hadn't figured out all the things cheechako meant. For openers it meant that he was new here, that his skin was white, that he didn't know anything about living in Alaska, and that as far as these kids were concerned, he ought to be leaving soon.

Abruptly, the piercing wail of a siren shattered the ticking-clock silence of the drowsy schoolroom. All but Will jumped to their feet, excitedly yanking on parkas and boots.

"What is it?" blurted Will, alarmed, shoving out of his desk.

CHEECHAKO

"What is it?" mimicked Phillip, Edwin's shadow, who sat across the aisle on Will's right. "It's Breakup. Don't you cheechakos know anything?"

"I know enough not to get excited about ice melting," Will said, but Phillip was gone. Breakup on the Tanana, Alaska's second-largest river, signaled the end of the long subarctic winter. When the siren blew, everybody in town dropped everything and ran to the river to watch and to celebrate.

One good thing, thought Will, puffing along behind the growing crowd, *maybe now we can get out of here.* He welcomed the idea of moving out to their new homestead, a move they couldn't make until the river ran clear of ice. "I hate the kids here," he had told his mother after the first month of school.

"Oh Will, give them time," she answered sympathetically as he helped her with supper dishes. "After all, you are an outsider. Maybe they're waiting for you to make the first move."

"What kind of first move can you make with people who want to fight you all the time?"

"It will get better," she said, rinsing a sudsy plate. "You'll see."

"They're not like the guys back home, Mom. We used to get together after school for a game of baseball, or go out for a pizza. Here, there's three feet of snow piled up on the baseball field—if you call that a field—and the closest pizza parlor is in Fairbanks...sixty miles away!"

"I was homesick when I first got here, too…" Mom began, but Will wasn't finished.

"These Alaska kids spend most of their time snowshoeing or driving dog teams or…or…hunting!"

Will paused to put the wet skillet on the cookstove to dry. He didn't know how to do any of those things but he was desperate to learn.

"They don't like me," he shrugged, "because I don't know anything. And since I don't know anything, they don't want to hang around with me. I can't win!"

As if that weren't bad enough, his folks had begun talking about boarding him in Nenana for another school year, of finding a family for him to stay with while the two of them went out to finish the homestead.

"I don't want to stay here alone," Will wailed. "I always get left behind!"

His real father took off when Will was a baby. Just two years ago, Jim married Will's mother, then moved them to Alaska. Now it seemed Will would be left behind again, this time by both his parents as they went out to improve the homestead.

The State of Alaska hired Jim, a wildlife biologist, to count migratory animals like caribou. He'd been out in the Bush now for nearly two months, but was due back any day. When he wasn't counting wildlife, he worked to finish their log cabin. To earn extra money, they planned to grow vegetables and sell them at the general store.

CHEECHAKO

"Please," Will had begged, "let me go with you."

"You're better off for now, staying in town where you can go to school and be around kids your own age," said his step-dad. "It's pretty lonely out there."

"You don't know how lonely it is *here*," Will said, straining to hold back tears. But he knew that wasn't the only reason he'd be left behind. He had over-heard his parents talking one night.

"This isn't Boston," he heard Jim whisper. "Will doesn't know a thing about life in the wilderness."

"But how will he learn," asked Will's mother.

"I'll teach him," said Jim. "In fact, I've been looking forward to the time we'll spend together out there. But with building the cabin and doing the game counts and all…" There was a pause.

"You haven't had the time to teach him. It's okay. I understand. And I know he'll understand, too."

"But it's not just that," Jim continued thoughtfully. "When we're out there together, we have to be able to count on each other. I'm not saying it's dangerous, exactly, but there's a lot that can go wrong. And up here, small things can kill you. I'm just not sure I could count on him if things got rough. But next year…"

As Will half-jogged with the crowd toward the river, he hated to think Jim might be right. If something did go wrong, could he count on me? He hoped so, but at this moment there didn't seem to be much proof. *I'll be a cheechako forever!*

As they reached the riverbank, sheets of river ice, some as huge as baseball diamonds, rose and fell, grinding and crushing into smaller pieces.

All eyes fixed on a large, green-painted tripod of peeled logs frozen into holes chopped in the ice. When the ice moved, a thin steel cable would tighten, stopping a special timing clock.

People all over bet on the ice breakup. The person holding the ticket for Breakup's precise day, hour, and minute won a bundle of cash: hundreds of thousands of dollars, in the famous Nenana Ice Pool.

Some years the tripod moved, tripping the siren, and in an hour or so the ice swept the river clean. Other years the ice shifted a little and then built up in a massive jam, increasing the pressure and the danger. Those years the river flooded, spilling icy water into the town.

"Sure glad I'm not out there on the ice," someone said.

Boy, me too, thought Will, as he turned to leave.

"Look, a dog," someone cried. "A dog is caught out on the ice!" Will slipped to the front of the crowd for a better look.

Not fifteen feet from shore stood a shivering, skinny black dog.

"Get a plank," someone shouted. Quickly they found a long smooth board, slanted it down to the unstable ice, and tried to coax the dog to safety.

Will's ears filled with the snap of the wind and the roar of the river, just as his heart filled with fear at the sight of those huge, gnashing slabs of ice. But his eyes met those of the little dog. She seemed confused and frightened by the shouts from the bank, as much as from the deafening ice flow, and wouldn't budge.

"Ahhh, let the river eat her," said a rough-faced man.

"No," cried Will. Quickly he darted through the fringe of crowd. The closer Will got, the steeper and narrower the plank looked, with the ice bucking and pitching a good ten feet below.

"Don't think, just go," he told himself. Taking an awkward leap, he slid feet first down the slippery plank to the roller coaster rise and fall of the river ice.

A quick glance back showed a blur of faces, all eyes on him. *Oh boy,* he thought, *now I've done it.*

Gingerly, he started toward the dog, arms out from his shoulders for balance. Abruptly, the berg dipped, filling Will's boots with icy water.

Will gasped. He pictured himself sliding into the river, pulverized by pieces of ice the length of railroad cars. But the berg rose and Will, who'd been too frightened to breathe, sucked in a breath and stepped forward.

His heart sank as he realized that the dog sat on an entirely separate section of ice, with another smaller piece between them.

"Blackie," he called, for he had already decided what to name her. "Blackie, come on!"

But the cry choked off as the slab dropped again, water rising past Will's knees to his thighs. But as panic began to squeeze Will's heart, the berg teetered up, lifting him into the clear again. "Can't feel my feet," muttered Will, stumbling ahead.

In the distance, the siren sounded again. With a new sense of urgency, he started for the dog. Above the noise of the wind, the ice, and the shouting crowd, Will heard his name and turned.

It was Jim!

Jim waved his arms frantically. "Behind you," he shouted. Will shot a look in the direction Jim pointed. As though in slow motion, a huge slab swept toward Will, sinking and covering all the icebergs in its path. A two-foot wave, pushed ahead by the monstrous slab washed past, soaking him to the waist, nearly sweeping him away.

At the last instant, Will grabbed the edge of this new, skidding berg as the old one disappeared beneath him in the deep, black freezing water. In a single desperate move, he half jumped, half rolled onto the larger, more stable ice floe and discovered that Blackie had done the same. Will grabbed her up in both arms and turned to run for the safety of the wooden plank but it was gone.

Will gasped. He now faced a sheer wall of timbers, a hundred feet downriver from the low place where he'd jumped, with the shouting crowd running along the bank a full ten feet above him. His mind raced, as he looked for a place to get a grip and hold on.

Thoughts of his mom flashed through his mind, of how stupid he'd been, of how he was going to be in such deep trouble. *But only if I can get out of here alive. Jim, where are you?*

Set into the wooden face of the dock were several graded slips where in summer, longshoremen could walk down to the level of the river to load cargo into small boats. It was at one of these low spots that Will had been able to slide down.

Out of the corner of his eye, Will saw the next one approaching. He crept as close as he dared to the edge of his ice floe, but it wasn't close enough. A three-foot channel of deep, swiftly flowing water separated him from the timber wall.

Then, with a mighty crack, the ice severed behind him, leaving him balanced on a tiny slab, too small to support both Will and the dog.

The berg began a slow forward roll, toppling Will, with Blackie still clutched in his arms, toward the roiling surface of the unforgiving river.

But instead of plunging into the frigid water, he felt himself suspended in air, soaked clothes dripping and water-logged boots tugging in the strong current. He was hanging by his parka hood, half strangled by the collar.

"Drop the dog," somebody shouted, trying to yank Blackie out of Will's arms.

"No," snapped Jim's voice, "let him be." Then other hands took hold, and slowly—it felt like forever—Will's rescuers swung him to safety.

Lying in the slush, his hands to his throat and gasping for breath, Will became conscious of the excitement crackling like river ice around him. The whole place had gone crazy with Blackie licking his face and the crowd shouting, pounding Jim on the back, and shaking his hand.

Scrambling to his feet, Will faced Jim who grabbed him and hugged him hard. "You've got guts," Jim said. "Now we've got to do some work on good sense. God! You gave me a scare!"

"So..." Will stammered, "I'm not in trouble?"

"Oh boy are you in trouble. You're grounded 'til forever. That was about the dumbest..."

An old man with a wrinkled face stepped up to Will. "You saved my dog. But it was a darn foolish thing you done. You got guts though, I'll give you that."

"Your dog," said Will, drooping. "But I was hoping..."

"My dog all right," said the man. "She's real valuable, a trained lead dog."

Jim read the longing on Will's face. "We don't have a lot of money, but..." he began.

"Not for sale," said the old man. But then his wrinkles clustered into a weathered smile. "She's yours, boy—a gift. A gutsy boy deserves a good dog.

"Th...thanks!" Will stuttered, suddenly finding it difficult to move his lips.

CHEECHAKO

"Let's get you home and out of those wet clothes before they freeze solid," Jim said, turning Will by the shoulders. "Your mother's gonna kill...at least one of us."

As Will turned to follow Jim back along the dock, someone blocked his path. It was Elias Charlie, a tough Indian kid from school. Tougher than Edwin. Will knew that Elias' father and older brother numbered among the state's top dogsled racers.

Half a head taller than Will, Elias had blue-black hair and a hawk-like broken nose. Right now he looked like trouble, but after the river, how bad could it be?

Here goes, thought Will, and drawing a deep breath, he stepped up to face the larger boy. For a long moment Elias stared at Will, expressionless. Then his face fell into a lopsided grin—as though it wasn't used to smiling.

"That's a good dog," said Elias, kneeling to pet her. "I know this dog. My uncle trained her." He started to speak again, then turned to look out over the river. "If you want," he said, "maybe I could show you how to hitch her up sometime."

Will was so stunned he had to remind himself to close his mouth. "Tomorrow?" he murmured, and the boy nodded.

All the way home, walking sodden streets with Jim and Blackie, Will felt different. Older, tougher, hopeful—maybe even 'gutsy'! Tomorrow he'd learn something about driving a dogsled, if he survived his mother!

CHAPTER 2

"Wait here." Elias disappeared into the shed where his father stored racing gear. After some banging and clattering against the corrugated tin walls, he emerged dragging a small, unusual dogsled.

"Wheels," laughed Will. "It has wheels."

It was the weirdest dogsled Will had ever seen. Even straight-faced Elias laughed a little. "Well, the snow is mostly melted, what did you expect?"

Actually Will hadn't known what to expect. He started out the morning helping his mother pack, running to the store for extra boxes, stuffing, taping and labeling them. Then the phone—which almost never rang—startled them both. Stranger than that, his mother picked up the phone, said hello, then handed the phone to Will. "It's for you."

"For me?" He mouthed the words silently, pointing at himself. It was Will's first phone call in nearly a year at Nenana.

A tentative voice said, "It's Elias." Will had the feeling Elias didn't use the phone much either. "Can you come over? I want to show you something."

"It's Elias Charlie, Mom," he said, trying not to look as pleased as he felt. "He wants to know if I can come over."

She looked doubtfully at the stacks of boxes and standing clutter.

"I suppose—for a while."

"Bring Blackie if you want," said Elias.

"Sure." He hung up the phone with his mother grinning at him, her arms out, palms up.

"Yeah, I know," he said. "You *told* me so."

* * *

Just five feet long, the dogsled had been built by Elias' Uncle Charles. He went by 'Charles' so people wouldn't call him Charlie Charlie. He did most of the sled building while Elias' father, Aaron Charlie, did the mushing.

"My uncle built this sled in our backyard," said Elias with pride. "I helped." He described the process of selecting straight-grained birch trees, falling them, and sealing the ends with tar to season for almost two years. "Slow drying is important so the wood won't crack and split," Elias added.

Next Uncle Charles rip-sawed the logs by hand into sled dimensions, steaming the pieces in a long, water-filled trough to make them easy to bend. He knew how to soak the moose hide laces and knot them wet so that as they dried, they'd pull the pieces tightly together.

Now, with the sled tied to a fence post, Elias brought out two large, excited huskies. It took both boys to get the harnesses on them, and get them clipped to the sled. They were ready to run.

Next, Elias rustled around in the dog shed until he found a smaller harness, which he handed to Will. "For Blackie," he said. "It's an old one—needs some stitching—my dad says you can have it."

Blackie stood stock still, but quivered excitedly, as Will slipped the harness over her head and awkwardly adjusted the bellyband. After Elias showed him how to clip her onto the front of the lead line, they stood back to admire the effect.

"How can she be a lead dog?" Will laughed. "She's half the size of the others."

"I've seen this dog work," said Elias. "These other dogs—we call them wheel dogs when they're right in front of the sled—their job is pulling. Her job is leading. You don't have to be big to be smart, and this one is smart." He gave the harness set-up one last, quick check. "C'mon," he said. "Jump in." Will didn't have to be asked twice.

"Okay," Elias called to his three-dog team, untying the sled from its anchor post. Ears up, yipping excitedly, the dogs headed down the slushy road.

"Gee!" shouted Elias. "Gee!" he repeated as the dogs approached a trail intersection.

"Gee-ee-ee?" Questioned Will from his bumpy seat on the hardwood slats.

"It means go right. Haw means go left," said Elias, running behind the sled, beginning to pant a little. "We'll see if she remembers."

She did. The small black lead dog made a clean right onto the trail, easily turning the two big dogs behind her. Running, she looked back over her shoulder, ears streaming in the wind and her pink tongue hanging happily out the corner of her mouth.

"Good dog, Blackie," Will shouted. "Good dog." And he settled back to enjoy his hard, bumpy ride.

For the next couple of weeks, while they waited for Jim to come back upriver with the boat, Will spent part of each day helping his mother pack, and part of it with Elias, learning—he hoped—to not be a cheechako.

To Will's delight, he quickly became an accepted member of the Charlie family dog-racing team. What he thought he was doing for fun, driving the dogsled with Elias, testing and training various lead dogs, turned out to be a real job. At the end of the first week, Elias' dad pressed a wrinkled ten-dollar bill into Will's hands, along with a fresh-caught river salmon nearly two feet long, and thanked him for his help.

Will beamed as he struggled home with his wages. *This fish weighs thirty pounds, if it weighs an ounce,* he thought, as he imagined the look on his mom's face as he presented it to her.

* * *

Monday morning early, the phone rang. "For you, Will," his mother called. "Elias."

Will staggered out to the kitchen in his pajamas. "Hello?"

"Want to work," asked Elias.

"It's six in the morning!" Will yawned. "I want to sleep."

"You can sleep when you're dead," said Elias. "Right now there are dogs to feed, and Andy's laid up."

Andy, Elias' second-oldest brother—who usually did all the dog feeding—had been splitting firewood when the axe slipped, slicing through his boot and into the top of his foot. The public health nurse stitched him up and told him to stay off it for two weeks.

"How many dogs," asked Will, almost afraid to hear the answer.

"All of them," said Elias. "Fifty dogs—give or take some new puppies."

"We'd better get started then," said Will. Hanging up, he went to find his work jeans and flannel shirt. "I'm feeding dogs," he told his mother.

"Feed yourself first," she said. "I have a feeling you're going to need it."

By the time Will made it down to the dog lot, Elias had a brisk fire burning, and was using a canoe paddle to stir something that was bubbling and frothing in the cut-off half of a steel drum.

"Smells like fish," said Will, wrinkling his nose.

Elias grinned. "Stinks, doesn't it. That's what the dogs like about it. Fish heads, old moose bones, and lots of oatmeal. This is the secret to all our wins: fish porridge. It smells so bad if they didn't eat it, they'd want to roll in it. Want some?"

"No thanks," said Will, eyeing the concoction. "I already ate."

All around them on the large open lot, stood rows of unpainted wooden doghouses, built with simple, nearly flat roofs, most with a dog standing on top. In front of each house was a pair of battered tin pans for food and water, and a sturdy pole where the dog's steel chain attached.

Elias handed Will a bucket and a large spoon. "Two scoops for each," he said. "Don't try to pet these dogs 'til they know you, and watch out for the chain when they rush the food bowl—which they will." He pointed with his spoon. "You go that way."

As he made his way down the row, slapping a spoonful of the fish mush into each pan, Will found himself studying each dog's face. They were all mixed-breed, so no Labradors or Golden Retrievers, or any of the kinds he'd been used to back east. But although every dog was different, he found himself realizing that most of them had one thing in common. They all looked like wolves.

There were black faces, brown faces, and white faces with wolf-like masks in contrasting colors. Some of them had a colored spot over each eye, which looked like eyes that were always open, even when they were sleeping. There were short tails, long tails, bushy tails—and they were all wagging.

Some had ears that stood sharply erect, while a few had hanging, flappy ears. Some had one ear up, and the other only half up, not that any of them could hear much with all the racket.

All around they were in motion, barking, yipping, and howling their excitement about breakfast.

With the food all distributed, Elias and Will circled the lot with a wheelbarrow, carrying a water tank fitted with a spigot and hose. Each water pan had to be turned right-side-up and filled with clean water. The entire feeding and watering took more than two hours.

"Tonight will be easier," said Elias. "No cooking; we just toss them half a dried fish. Much quicker and easier. So..." He looked sideways at Will. "I told my dad we could do this job together 'til Andy can walk. You and me. We'll make some easy money. Okay?"

"Okay," said Will, inwardly stunned at Elias' notion of dog-feeding as "easy" money. But he wasn't about to back out of a chance like this with his new friend. The truth was, after several hours of dog care, he was tired, sweaty and ravenously hungry. "I'm starving," he said.

"Me too," said Elias. "Feed me or shoot me! That's what my Auntie Ruth says."

Will laughed. "I'm for feeding," he said, and the two boys went off in search of something more appealing than fish porridge.

* * *

As they carried the last two boxes from the pickup, Elias asked Will again about the homestead site. Will paused and looked out at the long, flat-bottomed riverboat, fully loaded with the family's household goods.

He grinned. "Same as the last time you asked me. About twenty miles down the Tanana, where the river makes a wide curve east. Why?"

Elias shrugged. "Just making sure you cheechakos know where you're going. I wouldn't want to have to come out and rescue you."

Will laughed. It was the first time he'd laughed at being called a cheechako. He was conscious of Elias, smiling, watching him laugh. It felt good to have a friend.

"Cast us off, Elias," called Jim. He was standing in the back of the boat by the outboard; there'd been a place left clear for Will to sit, with his mother and Blackie closer to the bow. With everything aboard, they were waiting only for him.

"Well," said Will, "see you." He said it cheerfully, but inside he already missed his friend.

"Yep," Elias said, grinning.

Watching the sandy shore slide by, the muddy water and stands of willow, black spruce, and birch, Will felt a rising sense of excitement. Even though he'd never been there, he turned to his mother and Jim, shouting over the roar of the kicker, "It feels like we're going home."

* * *

The cache was Will's first experience building something completely from scratch.

"Most folks build above sea level," Jim laughed. "We're building this cache above bear level."

After his year in Nenana, Will knew an Alaskan cache when he saw one: a small, windowless log cabin built ten or twelve feet off the ground to keep bear and wolverine out of the food supplies.

"Why call it cash," asked Will, "unless miners used to keep their money there, too?"

"Not c-a-s-h cash," said Jim, "but c-a-c-h-e cache. It's a French word, I think. Sounds the same, but means a place to hide or stow supplies. We're going to be very happy we have this next winter when the snow flies and the animals come sniffing around for snacks. First we build it, then we fill it. Then we're ready for winter."

To get logs, they traveled a few miles upriver, because the best trees nearby had already been harvested for their cabin. Will helped Jim select and fall the straightest, tight-grained spruce, six to eight inches in diameter. He learned to operate the chainsaw by limbing the logs and bucking them into workable lengths. After that, he rolled them to the river and roped them tightly into a raft for the trip home.

"Will...get down," Jim whispered urgently, pulling Will into a crouch. He pointed. "Look over there."

As Will watched, first one wolf and then another, his mate, stepped cautiously from the undergrowth, padding shoulder-to-shoulder toward the riverbank.

Will had spotted plenty of wolves since moving to the homestead but none like these. These were the biggest he'd seen, and instead of gray or brown, were nearly black, with a distinctive spray of yellow-rust at the shoulders and along their sides.

"I've never seen wolves like these in this valley," Jim whispered excitedly. "And nobody else has either. Not since the turn of the century, anyway. At least nobody who reported it. They're usually spotted quite a bit north and west of here...if at all."

"Did you bring your camera?"

Jim nodded toward the boat. "I brought it, but it's not going to do us much good. They'd be gone before I could even get my hands on it."

"What can we do?"

"Just look at them. And remember them. What you're seeing, few have seen and even fewer will as time passes. I'd hate to guess how long those wolves might survive in this valley without somebody getting an idea of what those hides might be worth. Just remember them," he repeated, almost reverently.

For about twenty minutes, the wolves waded in the shallows and drank, then climbed the riverbank and headed back toward the brush. The pair moved slowly, almost confidently, as though this was their land and they were in charge. Just before disappearing from view, the male turned to stare directly at Will and Jim where they crouched. In another second, both were gone.

Few words were exchanged as they gathered the last of the tools, loading the boat in preparation for the trip back downriver. Will felt very lucky and grateful for having seen the wolves. He hoped their image would remain fresh and vivid in his mind for a long, long time.

Instead of taking his usual place in the bow of the boat, Will asked if he could drift the raft back while Jim motored ahead. A steady breeze kept the bugs off, and he felt like Huckleberry Finn, sliding silently down the broad, smooth river, through the summer twilight that passes for darkness in the land of the midnight sun.

* * *

"How big is a cord?" Will asked. Sawing, splitting and stacking next winter's firewood had become his job while his mother managed their huge garden and Jim scrounged such things as logs and floating river scrap to construct a rambling tin-roofed shed.

"A cord is big," Jim replied cheerfully. "So keep chopping."

"But I need to know how big," Will persisted. Sawing, chopping, sweating, and raising a fresh crop of blisters right through his work gloves, it seemed important to know what he was in for.

CHEECHAKO

"Alright," said Jim. "A cord is a stack of firewood four feet high, four feet wide, and eight feet long. I'm guessing we need about four cords to make it through the winter."

Will surveyed the half of one pile he'd split and stacked so far, and sighed. "Looks like a long summer."

"It would go quicker if you could find a helper," said Jim mysteriously.

"Sure, a helper out here in the woods."

Jim laughed and pointed behind Will.

"Elias," Will shouted. "What are you doing here?"

"Howdy cheechako," said Elias, tossing his bedroll aside to pick up the spare axe. "I heard you needed someone to show you how to make wood, so I came over." Elias waved toward the river. His dad was just nosing their long boat out into the current. Will hadn't been able to hear the outboard over the racket of the chainsaw.

Will couldn't help grinning. "You came all the way from Nenana?"

"Nah, from fish camp, about ten miles downriver. My dad has to make a run back to town, so he'll pick me up when he comes by tomorrow. That's why I kept asking you where your place was, 'cause I come out here every summer. Heck," he said, smoothly splitting a chunk of wood. "We're practically neighbors."

The two boys spent the rest of the afternoon splitting and stacking firewood, finishing the first cord and more than half of the second.

Will quickly copied Elias' roundhouse swing. Instead of simply raising the axe and letting it fall, he'd start the axe low at his side, completing a full circle with the axe head before it struck the round. The extra force usually split the dry alder or spruce clean apart. Sometimes it didn't. It was one of those times that Will, struggling to remove the stuck axe head, realized that Elias had stopped splitting and stood watching him. He fumbled and struggled all the harder but it was no use.

Elias made a clucking sound. "You cut wood like a white man." Grabbing the handle end, he gave it a sharp yank, the single motion popping the axe head free.

Hot and tired, feeling a little foolish, Will was not in the best mood. He'd been working hard, as hard as he could. Now he felt his face flush angrily.

Elias held up his hands, grinning. "Alright, not as bad as a white man. Look here," said Elias, "you've got to read this log." He pointed to the grain end. "My dad used to ask me, 'Do you hit where you aim or aim where you hit?'"

"Huh?" said Will, not following Elias at all.

"You're hitting this log any old where. That's the hard way. My dad showed me how to find the little crack, called a check." Elias touched a spot on the chunk of wood.

Will squinted at the crack. It was almost too tiny to see, let alone hit.

"The wood wants to split along this line, so all you have to do is hit it. It'll split easy if you hit where you aim. Try it."

Will didn't much like the idea of Elias seeing him screw up. "I don't see how it can make that much difference," he said, then swung with all his might.

He nailed the check dead on, and the wood split so cleanly, that the axe head embedded itself in the chopping block below and wanted to stay there. Grabbing the axe by its handle end, Will tried giving it a clean, sharp yank, as he'd seen Elias do. It popped loose. "Alright!" crowed Will.

After dinner, and after clearing and washing the dishes, the boys slathered themselves with mosquito repellent and headed back outside. The mosquitoes dive-bombed them in a black cloud, buzzing hungrily. Elias didn't seem to notice but Will couldn't help swatting at them. "These are the biggest mosquitoes I've ever seen!"

"If they're bothering you," said Elias, "just put rocks in your pocket." It seemed a little strange to Will, but he'd already learned so much from Elias he was willing to give it a try. For the next few minutes he and Elias searched the sandy soil as Will filled his pants, shirt, and jacket pockets with small rocks. Then he waited to see what would happen.

"I don't see any difference," he said finally. "Are these rocks supposed to keep mosquitoes away?"

"No," said Elias, "but rocks make it harder for them to swoop down and carry you off."

Will felt pretty stupid, standing there covered with mosquitoes and all his pockets jammed full of rocks. But he grinned sheepishly and laughed.

That night, they tossed their bedrolls into the empty cache and clambered up. After thumb-tacking mosquito netting to the doorframe—and smacking the ones trapped inside—they shucked their boots, jeans and jackets and bedded down.

Lying on their bellies with their heads near the open doorway, they could see across the top of the cabin to the river. In the half light, a huge moose grazed among the willows.

"Geez," breathed Will. "It's huge. Bigger than a horse."

"Yeah," said Elias. "His antler spread's at least five feet. He'd make good eating."

"You ever shoot a moose," Will asked.

"Sure."

"Cool," Will sighed.

"You ever been to a Yankee's game," Elias asked.

Will grinned at his friend. "Yeah."

"Cool!"

They watched and talked until Will closed his eyes, just to rest them, and then it was morning.

"Watch this," said Elias. Spreading his stance he let fly with Will's kindling hatchet. Spinning end-over-end, it bulls-eyed, blade first into the butt of an alder log.

"Wow," said Will. At first he was impressed, but remembering last night's pockets full of rocks, he became skeptical. "Bet you can't do it again."

"Bet I can," said Elias, and proceeded to stick the hatchet in the same log end, almost in the same split, four more times in a row. "Now you try it," he said.

Will grasped the hatchet by the handle and yanked it free. Walking back to stand by Elias he tested the balance of it in his hand. Suddenly, the hatchet had changed from an ordinary, sort of boring tool, into something interesting.

"Better step up a bit," said Elias, and walking a few paces toward the woodpile, he toed a straight line in the sand. "Right here."

Drawing his arm back from the shoulder, Will sent it spinning toward the log end. Rather than the satisfying 'thunk' he'd come to expect from Elias' throws, his made a kind of rattling, clattering sound and skittered back across the woodpile to disappear among the logs. By the time the boys got the wood unpiled, recovered the hatchet and repiled the wood, they heard the drone of an outboard approaching.

"That's my dad," said Elias. Quickly he scrambled up into the cache for his bedroll, then sprinted to the cabin and popped his head in the door. "Thanks for keeping me," he said to Will's mother and Jim.

"Race you to the river," he called to Will, and the two lit out for the sandy shore, arriving in time to catch the bow line as Elias' dad nosed the boat in. Will managed a poor second in the race, his heart thumping and his lungs burning. "Guess I'm not in very good shape," he muttered, breathless.

"You will be," said Elias. "That's what life in the Bush does for you—makes you tough." Knuckling Will in the arm, Elias vaulted easily into the boat.

"Now it's your turn to visit me," he said. "Ask your folks if you can come to fish camp for a couple of days. We'll have hatchet-throwing contests," he promised, "and I'll teach you to gut fish."

"Gut fish?" said Will.

"That's my job," said Elias. "That's why we call it fish camp. He laughed at the look on Will's face.

"I'll be there," said Will. "If you can gut fish, I can gut fish." Elias' grin told him he'd said the right thing. Pushing the boat out into the current, he stood waving until his friend disappeared from view, then returned to his woodpile.

"Cutting wood was more fun when Elias was here," he told his mother. At least now it didn't seem as hard.

At supper, he popped the question about visiting Elias at fish camp.

"Sounds like fun," said his mother.

"Terrific," said Will. "When?"

"Just as soon as you finish the woodpile."

"Aaaah..." moaned Will. "Can't it wait?"

"Not in Alaska," said Jim. "In two or three months it will be thirty-degrees below zero—too cold and snowy to cut wood. Nope. Winter wood comes first."

Now that Will had a good reason to finish, the job went even quicker. As one week turned into two and then three, the woodpile steadily grew and hard calluses replaced Will's blisters.

At the same time, what his Mom affectionately called baby fat melted away, revealing lean, ropey muscles.

Will didn't know what was happening at first. His jeans kept sliding down over his hips. With his pocketknife, he had poked first one extra hole in his belt, then two more. He discovered he could work through the day, then path-find and romp with Blackie through the long Alaskan evenings—even after filling in all the holes and replanting plants in his Mom's garden that Blackie had so joyously dug up.

"If she pulls a sled nearly as well as she digs," Mom said, "you've got a champion on your hands."

In his spare time, Will worked to master the art of hatchet throwing. It looked so easy when Elias did it. At first Will had thrown twenty or thirty times before being rewarded with even one of those satisfying thunks and the sight of the hatchet stuck solid in the stump.

"Let me show you how to do that," said Jim one evening, after he'd sat smoking his pipe, watching for a spell.

Grabbing the hatchet in a meaningful way, he tested its balance in his hand. Puffing a cloud of smoke he said, "I think you're spinning it too much. You've got to rotate this baby through the air..." He drew back. "...scientifically," he said, and gave it a toss. The hatchet hit on its handle and skittered off into a bush. "So much for science," muttered Jim sheepishly.

Will laughed. It made him feel better knowing that Jim couldn't make it stick either—but not much better. "I don't know if I'm gonna be able to get the hang of this," he said to Blackie, who trotted happily back and forth with him to retrieve the hatchet.

Testing the hatchet balance in his hand, he tried imagining it turning once only on its way to the target. Then, drawing his arm full back, he let fly.

A few moments fix like photographs in time, and this was one of them. Will savored every detail. The strong, smooth pull of his arm and shoulder muscles as the hatchet came around, the tight-grain hickory handle sliding cleanly from his fingers, the yellow glint of sidelight winking on the dull-metal head as it made its perfect single turn, and the solid, echoing *ker-thunk* as it struck, dead center.

"Yes!" shouted Will, running to wrest the hatchet from its solid purchase in the stump. Blackie leaped and barked around him, sensing his excitement. *But can I do it again? After all*, he thought, *when you throw a hatchet a thousand times, it's bound to stick on a few.*

Standing back, he once again gripped the handle, imagined its single rotation, hauled back and let it fly. Bulls-eye!

CHEECHAKO

* * *

As Jim backed the riverboat into the current, Will stood with his bedroll and backpack on the sandy shore, facing the fish camp. The buzz of activity hesitated and all in the camp turned to get a look at their visitor. The adults' attention quickly returned to fish preparation and, after a few moments of staring shyly, a wave of younger children washed down the shore toward Will.

At the back of the wave Will caught sight of Elias ambling with hands in jeans pockets, his familiar face decorated with a broad grin. As the smaller children jostled each other for the privilege of carrying his gear, Will walked with Elias up through the camp.

"I've never seen so many fish," said Will. Elias glanced at the drying racks proudly.

"This is the best catch I've worked." He looked at Will carefully. "I hope you meant what you said about cleaning fish, because I'm having a hard time keeping up."

"Sure," said Will. It was great to see his friend again. Although he'd never cleaned fish before and hadn't been excited about the prospect, right now it seemed worth a shot.

"Come on," said Elias, "I'll show you around."

They began at the fish wheel. Tied up along the shore, the wheel turned, driven by the river current. Two large chicken-wire baskets scooped fish from the river.

Although Will had seen quite a few fish wheels from a distance, this was his first chance to walk the plank out from shore and actually stand on one. As they watched, the wheel turned up a large, wriggling silver fish, sluicing it neatly into a wooden box at one side.

"Wow," said Will, peering in. "This box is almost full."

"That's why I'm getting behind. I already emptied it once this morning."

Elias pointed. "That's a king salmon."

Will stepped closer to admire the great fish, gasping, dying. He fought the urge to toss it back into the river.

"I always feel sorry for the fish," said Elias, as if guessing his thoughts. Dad says creatures have spirits, too.

"Fish too?"

"Everything."

"But that makes it harder, doesn't it?" said Will. "How can you kill something if you think it has a spirit?

"To eat," said Elias. "Without these fish, and a moose or two, we wouldn't make it through the winter." He made a face. "I guess it sounds a little stupid, but I sort of talk to the fish in my head. I say 'thank you, fish, for keeping us alive through the winter.' And I try not to leave them here to suffer."

Picking up a sawed-off piece of baseball bat, Elias gave the fish a solid whack and it lay still. "C'mon," he said. "We don't have much time."

It didn't take much time to tour the fish camp. From the fish wheel, they advanced to the cleaning tables, then to drying racks laden with fish, split lengthwise to the tail, hanging over alder saplings. "This dried fish is for the dogs," explained Elias.

"And this is the 'people' salmon," he said as they entered the smoke house, filled with alder haze and the aroma of curing salmon. Will's mouth watered.

"Over there, under the trees," Elias gestured toward a small cabin, "that's the winter cabin."

Last stop on the tour turned out to be a row of tent-like structures—canvas upper wall and roof atop a wood-framed floor—with plenty of mosquito netting. "This is where we sleep."

"Everybody?"

"Yeah, everybody here is related," said Elias. "So we're used to crowding in together. These are my grandparents, uncles, aunts, cousins. It's like a big family campout that goes on all summer. We work all day and sit around the campfire at night, swatting mosquitoes and listening to stories."

"What kind of stories?"

"Stories about the old days. What the old ones did when they were our age—but we better not try."

Approaching a weathered worktable, Elias handed Will a long, rubber apron and an eighteen-inch butcher knife. "Watch that knife—it's sharp," he said, and motioned to a wheelbarrow filled with salmon.

"Just grab 'em by the gills, like this, and toss 'em up on the table. Cut off the head like this," he demonstrated, "and toss it into that barrel. Next, you split it up the belly and hand it to me so I can gut it and scoop out the eggs. Later, when you're just about bored out of your mind doing that job, we'll trade and then you can be bored out of your mind doing this one."

For a while they worked, saying little. Will grunting as he tossed the heavy fish onto the table. In minutes his front— and from his hands to his elbows—was covered with fish blood and scales. "Darnedest thing," said Elias, "how my nose always wants to itch when I get like this."

One fish turned into another and another as Will gradually fell into the rhythm of fish cleaning. "What kind of stories," he asked.

"Huh," said Elias.

"Around the campfire."

"Oh yeah. My favorites are the hunting stories." He paused to swipe at the tip of his nose with his shoulder. "You know, usually about the ones that got away. But my father tells a true story on my great-grandfather, from back in the early days. Great-grandpa was not more than twenty when a white friend brought him his first rifle. They went out moose hunting, leaving the spears at home. They were hardly out of town when the friend's pack strap broke, and he stopped to make a repair while Great-grandpa went ahead on the trail. He didn't go even half a mile before he came face to face with a huge moose."

"Uh-oh...what happened?"

"The moose stared at him for a minute, then lowered his rack—it was five or six feet across—and charged. Even though my great-grandfather had never fired a rifle before, he knew how it was supposed to work. So he puts the rifle to his shoulder, carefully sights, then squeezes the trigger. 'Click' goes the gun—empty—he had found the moose so close to town he never even had the chance to load up.

"What'd he do?"

"The way my father tells it, he sort of dodged aside like a Mexican bullfighter. Holding the rifle by the barrel, he clubbed the moose to the ground before it could grind him up. Moose are huge. You know if you hit one with your car, the car's totaled."

"He knocked the moose down?" Will looked into the wheelbarrow. It was empty. "I'm out of fish."

"Good," said Elias, "we can take a break." He gestured to Will to follow and they headed toward the river to rinse off. "Anyway, after a bit the friend strolls up and sees Great-grandpa skinning out this moose. 'Well now,' he says—and he's very proud of this rifle—'now that you've tried a modern weapon, I suppose you won't be going back to that old-fashioned spear.'"

"Great-grandpa says 'Will still use spear.' The guy says 'But why?' Great-grandpa says 'Can always tell when spear is loaded.'"

* * *

"I don't understand why your family needs all this fish." Their break over, Will stood, knife in hand at the worktable, once again covered with fish blood, slime and glittering scales. In nearly four hours he'd already cleaned more fish than some sport fishermen do in their entire lives. He was hot, his back ached, and he hated the buzzing of flies drawn by fish blood.

Elias gave him a tired look. "We eat all this fish," he explained—a little carefully—as though talking to a child.

"Sure, I understand that…"

"No," said Elias, "you probably don't." Before Will could bristle, he continued. "Where you came from, everybody has jobs, they make money, and when they need food they go to the store and buy it."

"Right."

"It's different here. Even when we're living in Nenana we're really just living out in the woods. There aren't many jobs so there isn't much money and you already noticed there's only one store. The other thing is that my family has been moving up and down this river for hundreds of years catching fish, smoking and drying them to fill up the cache, feed the dogs, and live through another winter. You're about to find out what that's all about."

"What do you mean? I've already lived through one winter in Alaska."

"That was a town winter. You had a telephone and electricity. You had neighbors, the town nurse, and the fire department. Coghill's store was two blocks away and you could run over there in a couple of minutes if your mother ran out of baking powder."

"It's going to be different for you this winter. Anything can happen. The snow will be three or four feet deep—or more—and the temperature will be thirty or forty degrees below zero. There's no phone, no electric lights...no store." He paused, then looked sideways at Will.

"Grandpa says this will be a real hard winter. A storm winter, he calls it."

"How does he know?"

Elias shrugged. "He knows. He's lived through eighty Alaskan winters and here's the bad news: he says this is gonna be a bad one.

"You're kidding me, right? Setting me up to put more rocks in my pockets?"

Elias shook his head as he thwacked the head off yet another salmon.

"So what's the good news?" asked Will.

Elias looked into the wheelbarrow. "That was our last fish for today."

CHAPTER 3

Bundled in his puffy down parka and struggling through early twilight in the deep, drifted snow, Will hurried to finish his afternoon chores.

The first snow fell by the end of September, and the first blizzard before the end of October, and by now, late February, Will was beginning to think it might be this way forever.

"It's a storm winter alright," he muttered, bringing in a fifth awkward armload of his hard-split firewood. The wind caught his words, scattering them in a rattle of tiny ice particles against the frozen cabin wall. He frowned, forcing himself to keep his mind on firewood, and off the fact that Jim was now three long days overdue.

This wasn't like back in Boston where Jim might have only gone out to the grocery or maybe had a flat tire or stopped for a bite to eat. No, he'd gone out alone by dogsled at twenty degrees below zero to look for caribou. It was part of a special study to find out whether herds, which normally ranged farther north, might spend an especially cold winter in these more southern valleys.

CHEECHAKO

Now Will and his mother waited, snowbound, in their isolated log cabin, with the wind moaning, sighing and driving the drifting snow.

Will's moose hide mukluks crunched frozen snow as he trudged through the early dusk. Before they left Nenana, an old Athabascan woman called Grandma Susie had made them by hand. The mukluks reached almost to his knees.

He remembered visiting her one-room log cabin, smelling a smoky, delicious smell that turned out to be carefully tanned moose hide. Grandma Susie had him stand on a sheet of cardboard while she dropped heavily to her knees to trace the outline of his feet. It took nearly three weeks for the old woman to sew this pair, exactly to his measurements, and they fit perfectly. Will had to admit the mukluks did keep his feet warmer than the boots he'd been wearing.

Will's last chore of the day was to feed Big Runner and Blackie, the only two sled dogs left behind. He wished he could lose that nervous, twitchy feeling in the pit of his stomach. It would be great to see Runner and Blackie prick up their ears, to hear the joyous greeting barks of the in-coming team and to see the loaded sled with Jim loping behind.

Will stared at the two dogs expectantly, as though just having the idea could somehow make it happen. But Blackie only stared back and Runner sat down to scratch.

"I'll be back in seven days," Jim had said. "If I'm not back by then, well…" He looked from Will who, while stronger and tougher, still had little wilderness experience, to Will's mother, now eight months pregnant. "Well," he said again, "you'll have to come find me."

"Okay," said Will, excited by the prospect of a rescue mission. "I'll find you." But Jim just smiled.

It was the smile that irritated Will. He still doesn't think I have what it takes. That hurt because Will had worked extra hard to prove himself since coming out here.

"I can see you're fit," Jim went on, "but surviving in the Bush at twenty below requires more than just muscle and enthusiasm."

"*What* then?"

Tying a bundle of dried fish on the sled, Jim looked up. "You could call it a mixture of common sense and experience."

"Just the same, I think I could find you."

Jim thumped Will's shoulder lightheartedly. "Not to worry! I'll be back on schedule."

But he hadn't come back on schedule. "Not this time," said Will aloud, climbing the cache ladder. After tossing a frozen moose roast into the snow below, Will tossed down a couple of dried dog salmon for Blackie and Big Runner.

"Don't forget the orange juice," he said, reaching back into the cache. "One for each pocket. Oh, great, now I'm talking to myself."

Jim said talking to yourself is the first sign of cabin fever. Old-time miners and trappers, holed-up in their cabins so long, not doing anything, not thinking anything, not eating enough and often drinking too much, finally ended up doing more than just talking to themselves.

42

"It made 'em crazy. One old sourdough," Jim had said, "spent most of each winter, sitting in his bunk shooting at mice. And every summer he put a new floor in his cabin."

"He had that many mice?" Will had asked, amazed.

Jim chuckled. "He never had any mice."

Now, out of the corner of his eye, a flicker of light gave Will's heart a thump. Jim! But it was only his mother, placing a kerosene lantern in the tiny northern window, 'to guide him in.'

"Oh no," groaned Will, realizing what the lantern meant. He'd be doing his correspondence homework by candlelight tonight.

"Sarah's the penny-pincher in the family," Jim would say. It was his mother's job to balance what they earned, from the wildlife surveys and selling produce, with what they spent. So she never lit more than one kerosene lantern at a time, no matter what. She had a way of pressing her lips together when she made up her mind, and he could imagine her doing that now. That lantern would be in the window until Jim came home.

Climbing half-way down the ladder, Will cannon-balled the rest of the way into a chest-deep snowdrift, then floundered briskly back to the path which led to the cabin. "With all the other things I miss, like bakeries, showers, bicycles, and soccer games," he grinched, "I should get to miss homework, too."

"Will, where are you?" called his mother, standing wrapped in her parka by the cabin door. Her pregnant belly stuck out so far she could scarcely hold the edges of the parka together. "Will," she shouted again, and he could hear the edge of worry in her voice.

"Here, Mom, here, I'm coming," he shouted, and quickly shoveled a clean mound of snow for the dogs to 'drink'—water would freeze—and he loped back to the cabin. They went into the wanigan, quickly closing the outer door to save heat. Even so, as he opened the inside door, a chill white cloud of frosty air roiled across the cabin floor.

Will and his mother ate in semi-darkness. "An all-Alaska dinner," said Will, breaking the silence of eating and worrying. For a moment his mother's face softened, and they laughed together. Usually it was Jim who proudly reminded them of the meals that were prepared totally from food off the land.

"I could eat a whole moose," Will said. But he felt a little guilty for being so hungry while watching his mother pick at her dinner, sigh, and shove the plate aside.

The evening passed slowly while Will plugged away at his homework.

Every six weeks during the long winter, the mail plane landed on the river ice, delivering letters, magazines, weeks-old newspapers, lots of catalogs and any mail orders that had gone out with the previous load. They would also take a bundle of his homework assignments. Will looked forward to seeing the mail plane land and taxi on skis. But it wasn't because he was excited about getting his assignments back. It was the news they all craved.

The mailbag would be stuffed nearly to the top with rolled newspapers. Unwrapping them became a ceremony.

They'd stack them with the oldest on top, then sip hot cocoa or nibble popcorn as they read them all the way through in order. Will smiled at the thought of his folks, who liked to read their newspapers together. He pictured them stretched out on the braided rug, pointing to headlines, reading interesting bits out loud, and catching up with events in a world in which they felt happily out of step.

It wasn't as if they had no contact at all. Their powerful radio receiver pulled in news broadcasts from far-off and exotic places, like Seattle, San Francisco, and once, late at night, even Honolulu. During the summer, they could listen all they wanted, using the tractor to recharge the batteries. But in the winter, with the tractor shut down and stored in the barn, they limited listening to a short broadcast out of Fairbanks—the all-important Tundra Telegraph.

The 'T.T.' as they called it, broadcast personal messages and news, important to people who lived in the Bush. Will paused over his fractions to listen as his mom switched on the set.

The booming warmth of the announcer's voice seemed just too big for the darkened, cramped cabin. Will's eyes met his mother's. In the small light of the radio, she stood with her belly out, hands braced behind her waist, looking very tired, with deep-set lines of worry on her brow.

"To Arnie David, in Huslia," the announcer read, "your carburetor is back-ordered. They'll try to fly it out on Wednesday. To Sally Jimmie near Minto, your uncle Billy is okay but the airplane was totaled. And good news to Marty Jensen near Clear. Congratulations, it's a boy! Wife, Celia is doing fine."

Then the commercial started—something about a vacation to paradise. "I hoped we might hear some good news," Mom admitted, "that an airplane picked him up, or someone spotted him."

"You know what I think it is," said Will. "He's late because there's so many caribou out there and…" His mother waved him to be quiet and listen, which was okay because neither of them believed what he was saying.

"…three-day outlook includes temperatures rising to near zero as a storm front, originating in Siberia, drives south and east across the state, accompanied by high winds and greater than average precipitation."

"What?" said Will.

"Blizzard," Mom translated. She said it in a way that made the word hang and vibrate in a cabin that had gone suddenly silent. "It's a huge storm coming across the Bering Straits from Russia." Will shivered and imagined himself snuggling under his goose down comforter, waiting out the storm. But his mother shook her head as though to clear her thinking, and his, then pressed her lips together. "We've got maybe twenty-four hours," she said, "to find Jim."

CHAPTER 4

Morning came too soon and Will woke late. At nine o'clock, dawn was already a fiery ribbon along the southeastern rim of hills. Smelling breakfast, he rolled out of bed and headed straight to the table in his red wool long johns.

His mother set a heaping plate of pancakes, eggs and canned Canadian bacon on the table. Will ate quickly and went to dress.

He pulled on three pairs of socks, two pairs of pants and his moose hide mukluks. Beneath his hooded parka he layered several shirts and a sweater. He wore his over-size moose hide mitts the Indian way—tied to a braided harness over his shoulders so he couldn't lose them.

His mother snapped off the radio as he came back into the kitchen. She'd been listening for an update on the blizzard, but said nothing. The sandwiches already made and packed, she poured scalding tea into a steel Thermos, then pointed a warning finger at him. "Home by dark," she said.

"But..." stammered Will. If he hit the trail by 10:00, dusk was not more than five hours away. Not much time to find somebody at ten degrees below zero, with the wind rising and snow drifting.

"But nothing," said Mom. "Now listen, Will, here are the rules. Stay on the trail. Head for Jim's halfway shack. He has plenty of food and firewood there and," she paused, "first-aid supplies. If there is something wrong, he'll probably be there. And take this," she added, removing her rifle from the gun rack on the wall.

"But Mom…"

"Take it," she said briskly. "Use it like I showed you. She leaned to hug him over her pregnant middle. "I love you, Willie."

"Love you, too," he said awkwardly, hugging her back.

She laughed, her eyes bright. "I think my arms are shrinking." She quickly kissed the tip of her finger and tapped it on the end of his nose. "Be back by dark, and no later."

Will harnessed his two-dog team and clipped them to the loaded work sled. Stepping to the runners, he waved to his mom. "Mush!" he shouted, and they were away.

The first part of the trail headed roughly south, following the river, then rose gently toward what would become foothills. Close behind those foothills, like jagged white teeth, towered the mighty Alaska Range. It stretched spine-like across the lower middle of the state, including Mt. McKinley at the northern tip.

The trail, though drifted in places, formed a clean cut in the snow. Nenana people still called this the Mail Trail, as it hadn't been many years since mushers carried mail from Nenana by dogsled to surrounding villages. Now airplanes delivered mail but the trail remained, like a highway through the Bush.

For the first hour, Will made good time. But rounding a curve and emerging from a protective willow thicket, he found himself on the edge of a broad, windswept clearing. It looked like smooth sledding, and would have been, if the snow's crust had been thick enough to support them. On snowshoes or skis he might have slid over easily, but footing for the dogs was difficult. Will kicked at the crust then sank knee-deep trying to break trail for them. The passage was painfully slow and made his ankles ache.

Mushing northwest forced Will to meet the wind head-on. He squinted against particles of snow—tiny, stinging missiles the size of birdshot, driven on the rumbling, moaning wind. Will thought of a movie he'd seen about the tank corps in the African desert. But instead of sand, snow whipped, swirled and stung, dancing across the drifts in small, tornado-like williwaws.

Panting, sweating, and acutely aware of passing daylight, Will crossed nearly to the opposite side of the clearing—more than a mile he supposed—when he realized he was in trouble.

"I'm lost," he said. "No, I know where I am, but where's the trail?" Out in this open space, it had blown completely away. He stopped the dogs and climbed on the sled for a better view. Nothing ahead. He turned to look back across the clearing.

Will wished he'd paid more attention when he and Jim came this way a couple of months ago. Ahead, slightly to the west, the land rose to a slight hummock, then fell from view.

The trail could be there. Whistling up the team, Will changed course, plowing through deep, crusty snow one determined step at a time.

"There it is," Will shouted to Blackie and Runner as they topped the rise. Minutes later, Will gladly put the windswept clearing behind him, and headed west into a thicket of small, sheltering birches.

Refiguring his day, Will decided to use five o'clock as sunset. It was the time his mother expected him to show up, even though he knew the sun would be down by that time, with only twilight remaining. Since he'd been on the trail by ten, he guessed he had seven hours of running time.

Heck, he thought, *it's only ten miles to the halfway shack. That ought to be plenty of time to make the distance, find Jim, and head for home.*

But part of him wasn't so sure. *If anything goes wrong,* he admitted, *I won't make it in time.* Will pictured his mother setting the lantern in the window, waiting in darkness for him, too. With a shock, he realized the danger she and the baby would be in if neither he nor Jim made it back.

The trail stretched on, oblivious to Will's need for haste. Laboriously they climbed up and down rolling hummocks, quickly skimming frozen streambeds, mushing through endless, identical thickets of willow or birch.

He sensed the temperature rising with the distant approach of the Siberian front. He knew, even from his short time in Alaska, the temperature must rise to get snowfall.

CHEECHAKO

Suddenly, without direction from Will, the dogs came to a dead stop. "Mush!" shouted Will. "Mush!" But the dogs remained motionless, noses into the wind. "I said mush," he shouted again. The huskies moved forward but only at a walk.

Topping a low rise, Will saw what his team had already smelled, and reached for the carbine. Wolves—three of them—outlined against the leaden sky.

Will clicked off the safety and eased the rifle to his shoulder. If these wolves attacked, and Blackie and Big Runner were killed or injured, he'd never find Jim. For that matter, he'd be lucky to get himself home alive.

Sighting carefully on the closest wolf, he began to slowly squeeze the trigger. Then Blackie barked. "Crack!" went the carbine, but Will's target had moved. Instead of scaring the critters off, they lunged straight toward Will and the huskies.

But they weren't wolves. These were dogs bounding toward the sled, tails wagging, pink tongues hanging, smiling in their happiness at finding friends. They were Jim's dogs.

Shuddering at the mistake he nearly made, Will pulled the next live cartridge from the rifle, which emptied the firing chamber, and he re-set the safety. "By the way, Jim, I shot one of your dogs," he said, mocking himself in disgust.

Will dug in his pack for a dried fish for each dog. With an anxious look at the sky, they set off, Jim's dogs trotting behind. "I wish I had harnesses for you guys. We'd sure make better time."

Circling a thicket of stunted black spruce, Will stepped sharply on the sled brake. "Whoa," he called. He hadn't expected a fork in the trail.

Will had the feeling he should go right. Trouble was, he could see the trail's most recent tracks headed left toward the river and away from where the halfway shack should be.

"I don't get it." Shaking his head, he climbed back on the sled runners. "Haw!" he cried, urging the team left through the trees and toward the river.

In twenty minutes they were crossing a long, treeless clearing which he knew to be a river sand bar under the snow. Here, where the wind blew and the snow drifted constantly, someone had hammered down a series of willow branches tipped with fluorescent orange ribbons to mark the trail. Jogging along, Will counted six more markers ahead of him before they dropped out of sight, most likely where the trail fell to river ice.

Although Will was certain he'd never taken this trail before, and never mushed across this sand bar, the area seemed familiar, especially the way the whole scene nestled into an approaching hill. "I've been here before," he puzzled, but didn't know when, and abruptly, he didn't care.

An explosive geyser of icy water blasted head high, just a few feet from the sled.

Will knew a drenching in this cold would be fatal, but didn't get much chance to feel relieved that the spray had missed him. With a sickening crack, the ice let go beneath him. The sled quickly settled to ankle depth before Will could direct his tiring team to yank him to safety.

CHEECHAKO

He'd heard old-timer's tales of sudden winter wettings. Even in winter, the river flows beneath six or eight feet of ice. When the ice settles, water forces through cracks to the surface.

That explained the geyser. He'd been in no danger of falling into the river. This was just a big puddle on top of river ice. The water was only six inches deep, though it had scared the stuffing out of him when he felt the sled sinking. With his mukluks drenched, his feet would freeze fast.

He'd packed Jim's canvas work mukluks at the very bottom of the load. But stopping to unload the sled, and trying to change his already-frozen mukluks out here on the ice, would freeze his feet for sure. Even now, the shocking cold had turned to an unbearable ache.

He mushed up his team, jogging behind to force circulation in his feet. It wasn't working. His mukluks felt like ice blocks. The best he could do was climb on the runners and stay there.

He would have to quickly find a sheltered spot and use some of his emergency kindling to build a small fire to save his feet.

Will fought back fear by thinking of his folks. *They're depending on me.*

Then fear fought him back. He saw himself in a wheelchair, with stumps instead of feet. He imagined himself never playing basketball again—all the stuff a kid takes for granted. He could still feel his feet, but not much.

What do I do?

"Cheechako!" echoed in his head. "Little Cheechako." What would Jim do? What would Elias do? "Well, they wouldn't stand here waiting for their feet to freeze, that's for sure," Will yelled angrily, to keep from crying.

He felt a hot rush of anger at himself for acting like a cheechako. The anger sent a surge of warmth through his body, but not to his feet.

Blackie barked, and the dogs lurched forward. As the three loose dogs raced ahead, he wondered about his weary team's fresh surge of energy before he smelled it too. Wood smoke. To Will, it smelled like perfume!

"Good dogs!" With tails high and pink tongues lolling the team dragged Will and the sled into the Charlie fish camp.

Will shivered as he looked around the abandoned camp. With the tent frames bare of canvas, the smokehouse empty and cold—its door flapping in the wind—and rows of stark, snow-covered drying racks, fish camp looked like a ghost town. Only the central cabin showed any sign of life. A trickle of smoke rose from its rusty chimney.

Will didn't bother to knock. His frozen mukluks clunked on the plank floor as he crossed the single room toward the warmth of the woodstove.

Made from a fifty-gallon oil drum, the stove lay on its side in a cradle of wonderfully warm stones. Though the fire had burned low, a deep, even bed of glowing embers promised warmth for hours. The fire quickly rekindled when Will tossed in several three-foot lengths of seasoned alder.

On a metal shelf at the back of the stove sat a teakettle, full of hot water. Will dribbled it on his mukluks to free frozen laces and melt the ice. After he struggled out of the mukluks and several pairs of stiff socks, Will sat cradling his feet in his hands.

A quick look told him two things about the cabin's occupant. It wasn't Jim, and whoever was here hadn't gone far.

A 30-30 carbine leaned against a stack of wooden Blazo-box shelves. Through the window, Will noticed a good set of Yukon snowshoes, long and moosehide-laced, too valuable to walk off and leave, not to mention too useful in this weather.

The sight of a wolf skin, stretched and nailed to a section of plywood, stopped Will in his tracks. "Oh no," he breathed. Instead of gray with silver, or reddish-brown, this wolf had been near-black, with a scattering of silvery and rusty-yellow hairs over the shoulders and along the sides. A dime-sized bullet hole high on the neck made it plain what had happened.

Remembering the last time he'd seen a wolf like this, on a summer evening by the river, fear twisted his stomach into knots. "Don't let it be one of my wolves," he murmured in a hopeful prayer. "Who would shoot a creature like this—and why?"

Abruptly he roused himself, and stuffing his feet into his warm moosehide mitts, Will shuffled to the cabin's only window to search the windswept yard.

"No dogsled," he said, "and no dogs." Normally he'd expect to see a sled tipped up on its runner ends, leaned against the cabin or one of the outbuildings. Someone had been here. Where was he now?

I have a bad feeling about this, he thought.

A flash of movement at the far end of the yard caught Will's eye. Squinting against the brilliance of snow-reflected gray light, Will made out a dogsled, then the swish of a harnessed dog's tail. An entire team was just standing there, and by the look of them, had been standing in that spot for several hours—so long that the snow had rippled and drifted around them.

As Will watched, a low drift at the side of the sled moved. "That's no drift," he said, scrambling to find something to put on his prickling, burning feet. He snatched a pair of canvas work mukluks from a nail on the log wall and rifled the Blazo shelves for several pair of heavy socks.

Stuffing himself back into his parka and mitts he stumbled anxiously toward the motionless mound in the snow.

Upwind from the cabin and Will's team, these dogs hadn't picked up his scent. Will nearly reached the sled before they noticed him and set up a yowl.

All the way across the camp, Will dreaded what, or who he'd find lying on the ground. He'd seen nothing around the cabin to suggest that Jim had holed up here. Could it be Uncle Charles Charlie, or Elias' father, Aaron Charlie? Had one of them had a heart attack? What if whoever this turned out to be needed a doctor?

CHEECHAKO

As Will drew closer, he saw that whoever this was had managed to drag a canvas tarp and a down-filled bedroll from the loaded sled and bundle them under and around him for warmth, like a cocoon.

At the sound of the dogs barking and the crunch of Will's feet in the snow, someone peeled back a corner flap to peer out. Grimacing with pain, his face drained of color and his teeth chattering, Elias managed a stiff smile.

"I n-never thought a ch-cheechako could look so g-good," he said.

CHAPTER 5

"It's my arm," groaned Elias through chattering teeth. "I'm not sure if it's broken but I'm real sure it's stuck." Pulling back the canvas flap, he showed Will his wrist, pinned beneath the runner of the loaded sled. Will felt a prickle of fear. If the blood supply had been blocked, Elias' hand could be frozen.

"No," said Elias, guessing his thoughts, "it isn't as bad as it looks. See." With effort he moved his hand, which he'd wrapped in a long, green muffler. "The sled's resting on a root or something."

"What happened?"

"When I reached under the sled to check the brake lashings, the team bolted. Next thing I knew I had a sled parked on my wrist. You'll have to unload it to get it off me."

"Maybe not." Will grabbed a long spruce pole from a stack beside the smokehouse and swiftly levered the runner off Elias' wrist. Elias pulled his hand free and rolled stiffly to his knees, his injured arm tucked in close against him.

"You got here just in time," he said, pulling a hatchet from beneath the canvas flap.

"What were you going to do with that?" Will asked, shocked, guessing the answer.

"It's an old wolf trick," said Elias. Freeze to death or leave the leg. When it's this cold the blood freezes before you can bleed to death."

"Ugh," said Will.

* * *

In the cabin, Will wrapped Elias in warm blankets then stirred cocoa mix into boiling water melted from fresh snow.

Elias sipped his cocoa. "You don't have much time to find your step-dad before the storm hits," he said.

"Tell me about it!" Will retorted grimly. "Soon as I get you squared away, I need to get back on the trail."

"Not without me," Elias muttered.

Will considered this then decided to change the subject. "I saw the wolf pelt."

Elias grimaced. "Airplane hunters target practicing. They'd been chasing this wolf, a big female, cut off from her pack. Time I got to the riverbank, she's down and dead. What got me—her mate wouldn't leave her. The hunters made a bunch of passes trying to nail him, too. Finally they flew away. Next day he was still there and didn't leave until sometime during the night. When I saw he was gone, I went out on the river. I thanked her for the warmth of her hide like my grandfather does." Elias fell silent, then added, "Wolves mate for life."

Will thought bitterly of his real father. "Even humans can't always do that."

The two sat, deep in their own thoughts. Will finally broke the silence. "I thought you'd be in Nenana. What are you doing out here, ducking school?"

"Ha," said Elias, brightening. "I keep forgetting you're a cheechako. Actually it's an old tribal custom that brings me out here. My people call it 'spring vacation'. Since I was sitting around doing nothing, Dad said I should make a run up here. The Talkeetna Classic is next week and a bunch of his gear got left when we cleared out last fall. I think he left it here on purpose so he could send me back for it."

"Why would he do that?"

"He wants to make an Indian out of me." Elias breathed the steamy aroma of cocoa rising from the chipped, blue porcelain mug.

For a few minutes Will allowed himself to forget the approaching storm. With the wind sighing and moaning, and the cozy crackle of a fire in the stove, he didn't want to be anywhere quite as much as this cabin until the storm passed.

But the vision of his mother waiting, worrying, and Jim needing him, stirred him from his chair to where his socks, hanging in the intense heat of the woodstove, were already dry.

"I'm coming, too," said Elias.

"What about your arm?"

"I won't have any trouble riding with a bum wrist. You're going to be the musher."

"My sled won't carry you and my gear."

"We'll take my sled. Uncle Charles built it to haul freight. It has steel runners and a brake that would stop a train."

"But I'm only driving two dogs."

"Not now. I've got extra harnesses for those three dogs of your dad's."

"Will five dogs be enough for such a big sled?"

"No," said Elias. "We'll run all my dogs, too."

"Ten dogs!"

"Nine. We'll lead one as a spare."

"But the most I've ever driven is five," Will said doubtfully.

"Is your lead dog any good?" Elias interrupted.

Will patted Blackie, who thumped her tail. "She's real good," he said.

"Then you won't have any trouble."

"But..."

"I'm okay, see?" Flexing his hand, he tried to hide a grimace as he formed a cautious fist.

"Boy, I hope so." Tying his mukluks and shrugging into his parka, Will scraped a layer of ice from a windowpane and squinted out at the windswept landscape. "How bad do you think it will get?"

Elias closed his eyes and pressed the fingers of his good hand against his forehead. "I see temperatures near zero, ten to twelve inches of snow, winds gusting to sixty knots, near white-out conditions—no possibility of clearing for about three days." He opened his eyes and shrugged.

"How do you know this stuff?" Will asked. "Did your grandfather teach you to read weather, too?"

"Yes, and I'll teach you," said Elias, untying a small leather pouch from his belt.

"Ancient Indian wisdom, huh?"

"Nope." He handed Will a square black object. "Just turn the little knob. It's a radio."

* * *

With the sled unloaded and double-knotted to a pine post, Will assembled the rest of the team. Clipping one lead line to another, he stretched it straight out in the snow at the front of the sled, adding the extra length needed to hook up all nine dogs.

He started at the back of the team, nearest the sled, where the more rowdy dogs would least likely get into a tangle. He finished with Blackie at the head.

CHEECHAKO

When all the dogs were clipped to the lead, lunging, yipping and snapping with their impatience to hit the trail, Will beckoned to Elias. He came out of the cabin clutching his goose down sleeping bag, the wolf pelt, and dragging his duffel, which Will tossed on the sled. Elias climbed onto the sled and wormed into the sleeping bag so only his nose and eyes showed. "Can't get warm," he said, "but this should help."

With the gear and the spare dog loaded, Will stepped to the runners and slipped the knot from the snub post.

"Mush!" he shouted, then, "Blackie, gee!" Blackie steered the team to the right in a long smooth arc through the deserted fish camp. With a glorious burst of acceleration, the huskies stretched out their legs and hit the river trail running.

This is more like it, thought Will, feeling more hopeful about finding Jim and getting home before the storm hit.

"Thin ice," warned Elias, his voice muffled in the folds of the down bag. Will shouted to Blackie who quickly turned the team away from another icy soaking.

They were still crossing river ice when the sun pierced the overcast, reflecting from millions of ice crystals in the snow crust. At the same time, the wind died down a bit and the going got easier.

The team scarcely slowed as it climbed the riverbank on the far side. Even so, Will jumped off the runners to jog and push as he'd seen seasoned mushers do. No sense wearing out the team hauling a driver who could be helping. At the top, the trail cut through a small willow thicket, gradually bearing west and reconnecting with the old Mail Trail, where they turned south.

"How far to the halfway shack?" asked Elias.

"No idea," said Will. He was panting a bit but felt good. "Jim figures it's a six-hour run from our cabin. But he's running five dogs and a loaded sled. We should make it a lot faster."

A half hour out, Elias shouted over his shoulder. "There's one thing that worries me."

The sled topped a small rise, revealing a fork in the trail. Will stepped on the iron claw to brake the team.

"What is it?"

"Indians call it a fork in the trail," Elias replied.

"Tie the sled to that birch," he said, "and check each fork for trail sign."

"What am I looking for?"

"Any kind of track that says somebody's been out here."

Since the sled was exactly the width of the trail cut, Will waded off the trail, through thigh-high drifts. The left fork showed signs of passage, a sled and team, with drifted powder settled into the ruts.

"Headed which way?" shouted Elias from the sled.

"Headed south."

"Then it's the other fork."

"How do you know?"

"Well, I don't for sure. But some mushers still use this old trail, so the fork with the tracks goes someplace. That would make the other a hunting or trapping trail, which is probably where Jim is.

"That makes sense."

"Any tracks on that right fork?"

Will knelt in the center of the trail, where he noticed no sled ruts. But perfectly outlined in the lightly crusted snow, he found a set of dog prints.

"Tracks of one dog. A big one."

Elias sat up straighter. "Do this," he said. "Mark a point at the back of one footprint, and then scratch a line out from that point toward each claw mark and see if they line up." He craned his neck, as though he'd be able to make out the track Will was examining. "Well," he asked finally, "do they?"

"Uh, yeah. And here's another track, smaller. Must be two dogs," said Will.

"It's the same animal."

"Nah. It's a lot smaller."

"That's the back print. The front ones will always be larger, especially if the wolf is running. Running makes the feet and toes spread."

Will stood up quickly. "Why would a wolf come out of the woods to walk on a trail?"

Elias grinned. "Why would *you*?"

"Duh," Will snorted. Then he looked around cautiously. The idea of sharing the trail with a huge wolf made him uneasy. "Let's keep moving," he said.

Nearly an hour passed as they mushed along the hunting trail. The dogs settled into a steady rhythm of strong pulling. Will noticed the team felt as uneasy about sharing the trail with a wolf as he did. Keeping heads lowered and ears back, they took turns sniffing the breeze.

The trail, which had been smooth and nearly snow-free back at the fork, gradually became bumpy and drift-filled. The huskies were forced to break their own trail. The wind returned steady, insistent, always in their faces, driving tiny crystals of ice into Will's squinted eyes. The journey became slow, tedious work, dampening Will's early thrill at driving the big team.

Elias might have been dozing in the down bag, for all Will saw or heard of him. Sweating, grunting, pushing, he felt a trickle of irritation with Elias for snuggling in the bag, leaving him out there alone.

The trail ran a nearly straight line through thickets of stunted black, swamp pine.

Dipping to cross a small frozen stream, it then rose, angling to Will's right. As they rounded the base of a small hill, the wind let up and Will braked the team.

The absence of wind and motion made the silence roar in Will's ears. All he could hear in the crushing silence was the cracking of frozen trees. Elias thrust his shoulders out of the sleeping bag, throwing back his hood to listen.

Will glanced around nervously. Something moved, back on the edge of a small clearing. He didn't see it exactly, rather sensed the movement. Overcoming his impulse to reach for the 30-30, he forced himself to stand watchful.

"There's someone here," he said softly.

"Something," Elias whispered back.

The sound started low and mournful, growing louder and then very loud. Abruptly it ceased, leaving only an echo. Will found himself crouched behind his sled, hair bristling on the back of his neck.

"Wolf," said Elias, pointing.

Another howl. As intense as a siren in old war movies, and as eerie. Even in the deep snow, the echo hung in the hollow of the hill. Several of the huskies whimpered, straining on their lines, dragging the sled until Will leaned on the brake. The team clearly wanted to be somewhere else.

Cautiously, Will untied the leather lacing on the scabbard, pulling the rifle free. The wolf howled again, and Will trembling, levered a shell into the firing chamber.

"Wait," said Elias. "Something's wrong."

"You're telling me!"

"That's not what I mean. The wolf's in a trap. A snare maybe."

"What should we do?"

"Leave him."

"We can't leave him to freeze! It would be like leaving you with your hand stuck under the sled runner."

"If you want to help him, shoot him. Maybe we can come back for the pelt after the storm."

"Shoot him! Me?" Will couldn't imagine shooting an animal in a trap.

"Do you see somebody else around here with all his fingers working," Elias retorted.

"I don't know if I can," Will said.

Elias scowled. "Oh great. You don't have the guts to put him out of his misery, so you want to leave him to die slow in a trap. You're talking like a cheechako.

The word stopped Will like a slap, stinging his already wind-burned cheeks.

"Look," said Elias. "If he's been in that trap any time at all, his foot will be all torn up, maybe even chewed half off. Even if you can figure out a way to get him out, it probably won't save him. So the best thing you can do is shoot him."

"Maybe," said Will, "maybe not." Rifle in hand, he started toward the wolf. He wanted to get as close as possible without alarming it. A scattering of small spruce allowed him to advance from tree to tree without showing himself. Reaching the last of the trees, he got his first clear look. He gasped. It was the surviving black wolf—the biggest wolf Will had ever seen.

The biggest dog on Jim's team weighed about sixty-five pounds. He kept an old set of bathroom scales out in the shed. During the winter, to monitor their health and the amount of food they got, each week Jim picked up each dog and stepped onto the scales. It was Will's job to read the weight, and subtract Jim's 180 pounds from the total. This animal weighed about three times what those ordinary huskies weighed. Almost 200 pounds!

This wolf had stepped, not into a steel trap, but an old braided-wire rabbit snare. There was no blood and judging by the marks in the snow, the animal hadn't been here long. But caught by his left foreleg, his future was clear. He would either freeze to death, or as Elias predicted, chew off his foot. Slowly, Will raised the carbine and took careful aim at the creature, who stopped struggling and turned, meeting Will's eyes across the gun sight.

After a long moment, Will pulled the carbine from his shoulder and levered the chamber open. By removing the live shell, the rifle would have to be re-cocked to fire. Then he tromped back through the deep snow to the sled.

"It's a snare not a trap," Will reported, "and I don't think he's been there very long. It doesn't look like he's hurt because there's no blood." He sighed. "If not being able to shoot a tied-up wolf means I'm a cheechako, then I am. He looked at me and I couldn't pull the trigger."

Jonathan Thomas Stratman

"Alright," Elias smiled, "just call me cheechako, too. I couldn't shoot him like that either." Then his face grew serious. "But I have a plan."

CHAPTER 6

"That's your plan?" said Will. He said it again at Elias' back as his friend dug, one-handed, through the loaded sled.

"So I'm supposed to crawl up to that wolf and set him free? You're crazy! 'I'm here, Mr. Wolf. If you'll just not rip my throat out, I'll untie this wire and you can be on your way.' How am I supposed to do that?"

"In disguise," said Elias. He thrust the black wolf pelt at Will.

"What am I supposed to do with this?"

"We'll tie it on you," said Elias, as if that explained everything.

In minutes they had the pelt rolled out flat and tied to Will's back.

"Lucky," said Elias with the job complete, cradling his sore wrist.

"What's lucky?"

"This being the mate to the dead one. Same black coat with rusty shoulders." He stroked the pelt. "Until now, most of the wolves I've seen were sort of brown or gray."

"So, because I look like family, he won't kill me?"

"It's the scent," said Elias. "That's what'll keep him from killing you." He hesitated a long moment. "Maybe."

"How do I untie that snare?"

"Cut it and it falls off. Tension on the wire is what keeps it tight. Then drop flat and hold still. The wolf should run away."

"What if he doesn't?"

Elias picked up the carbine and looked anxiously at the sky. "Then we end up with two wolf pelts and a lot of wasted daylight."

As they stealthily retraced his path through the snow, Will thought of all the ways this could go wrong.

"A wolf that size could kill me," he hissed over his shoulder. He wondered how well Elias could shoot. "A bullet could kill me. You know," he whispered, "this is a pretty stupid idea."

"I thought you'd like it," Elias whispered back.

"Why?"

"Aren't you the guy who went out on break-up ice to save a dog? This plan is a lot safer than that one."

At the last small spruce, Will turned to his friend. "You *are* a good shot, aren't you?"

Elias grinned and crossed his eyes. "Trust me."

"Why doesn't that make me feel better?" said Will, starting toward the wolf, trying not to let Elias hear his teeth chatter.

The wolf had been straining and jumping at the steel tether. Will could see blood along the animal's jaws and lips, from chewing at the wire. As Will crawled from the cover of the trees, the wolf stood stock still, legs stiff and quivering.

A slight breeze against Will's cheeks told him he was upwind, and the wolf couldn't pick up his scent. Closer, Will crawled, and closer. The wolf growled low in its throat. Will hesitated, then continued more slowly, as low to the ground as he could get and still crawl.

Almost to the wolf, Will paused, and in that silence heard the slow, ominous sound of the carbine cocking, twenty feet behind him.

Will glimpsed long, deadly canines revealed in a snarl beneath turned-back lips. Those teeth could rip the throat out of a moose calf as quickly and effectively as a knife. Will swallowed hard. Just a few more feet and he'd be within range.

It would be easy right now to stand up and walk away. A part of Will wanted to very badly. But standing up was just another way of saying, "Okay, shoot him."

The wolf threw his whole weight into a lunge at Will, yelping as the snare line snapped tight. The wire bit into his flesh, spraying a fine mist of very red droplets on the very white snow.

Reaching the wolf-trampled snow, Will thought of his mom and Jim. What if, in the middle of everybody needing him, he got himself killed by this wolf, who also needed him?

The wolf stood, taut, his front legs slightly forward and out from his body. His hind legs, looking too long, were bent in a half-crouch, as though ready to spring. He growled again, but Will saw no toothy snarl. In fact, as Will watched, the animal's thick black brush of a tail began a slow semaphore back and forth. Will wondered if wolves ever made a kill with their tails wagging.

Even through the pelt, Will felt the wolf's nose brush his shoulder, and he could hear the aggressive rush of air through its nostrils. As he moved in, nearly under the animal, the growling stopped. The wolf reared back on his hind legs and threw himself on Will.

The impact of the huge animal smashed him flat to the snow. He imagined Elias, seeing the attack, desperate to make a difficult shot without hitting him. Will wrapped himself in a ball to offer less for the wolf to bite. But he was in more danger of being licked to death.

Yipping and whining, spinning on its short tether, the wolf scampered, pranced and wriggled in a paroxysm of glee. His short, sharp barks had a happy ring and the great face was transformed with a husky-like smile.

CHEECHAKO

It's working, thought Will, trembling with relief. He thinks I'm his mate. The last few seconds, had been tough ones, waiting for either the bite or the bullet.

The wolf's obvious joy at being reunited with his mate dashed Will's momentary good feelings. In spite of trying to help, Will felt a little guilty for tricking the wolf, and a lot scared about what he would do when the wolf discovered it.

Will began searching for a firm place to chop the braided wire. All the while, the wolf pranced like a puppy, nudging Will with his nose, trying to play.

How long before he picks up my scent, Will wondered as his fingers followed the snare wire under the snow, over a fallen length of log. Still lying flat, Will swung the hatchet several times, unsuccessfully. Then he reared up on his knees, and whacked the wire hard, cutting it, and quickly ducked back.

After briefly gnawing at the severed snare, the wolf flung away the wire remains, as though ridding itself of a bitter taste.

Turning to where Will cowered, the wolf barked coaxingly, impatient to be gone, and pushed under the pelt to drag a long, wet tongue across Will's cheek.

I may smell like a wolf, thought Will, but I know I don't taste like one. The wolf's happy yips turned to a spine-chilling growl.

Will curled himself into the smallest possible ball. He still hoped to get out of this without being deliberately bitten or accidentally shot. But those early growls sounded like love poems compared to the sounds of rage the wolf made now. Will squeezed his eyes shut and waited for pain.

That's when the wolf charged Elias.

CHAPTER 7

Elias found himself faced with shooting the animal Will had risked his life to save. With the wolf advancing, snarling and only about twenty feet between them, it seemed he had little choice but to fire.

Gingerly supporting the rifle with his injured wrist, he aimed at the animal's broad chest, as he'd been taught. He took a deep breath, held it, and began ever-so-smoothly to squeeze the trigger. But running behind the wolf, in direct line of fire, came Will, still wearing the pelt.

To miss Will, Elias jerked the rifle skyward as it fired. Startled, the wolf stopped, yipped, then whirled sideways, as if knocked for a loop by the reverberating thunder. Still in danger of hitting Will, Elias did the only thing left for him to do. He turned and ran.

Protecting his 'mate', the wolf quickly closed the distance between himself and his enemy. Even in deep snow, he had a smooth, powerful gait.

In search of a tree large enough to climb, Elias stumbled down a short, steep incline to a snow-covered stream. He heard sharp cracking sounds beneath him as he crossed its frozen surface, but didn't dare slow down. Quickly he made the other side, only to flounder in deep snow. Having cornered him, the wolf began a slow menacing advance across the ice.

Regretfully, Elias made his apologies to the wolf and aimed, pulling the trigger just as the charging wolf crashed through the thin ice and disappeared.

Will burst from the brush at the stream's far side. He took in the situation at a glance. "It's below zero," he shouted, "how could this ice be thin enough to break?"

Elias looked around, getting his bearings. "Hot springs," he shouted, "just up there—watch out."

The wolf surfaced, thrashing. Dog-paddling desperately from side to side, he tried to find a place to haul himself out.

"He's a goner," said Elias. "I don't think there's anything else we can do but shoot him. A couple times there, I thought we might be able to save him."

"We've got to get him out," Will insisted.

Elias carefully threaded his way around to where Will stood on the ice, still wearing the wolf skin. With his good hand, he grabbed Will by the parka sleeve and hauled him around. "If we get him out, if we somehow manage to, what can we do besides shoot him, to keep him from killing us? Got that one worked out?"

The ice beneath the boys cracked ominously and Elias quickly yanked Will backwards. Will clawed his muffler from around his neck while shedding the clumsy pelt. "Grab my feet." Stretching full length on the ice, he tossed the muffler like a lifeline toward the wolf.

"I can't hold you with one hand!" shouted Elias in frustration.

Will's first throw fell short. The animal snapped at the muffler, but missed. In spite of everything Will and Elias had risked, the wolf was just as trapped as he'd been in the snare, and just as dead if they couldn't help him.

"A little farther," muttered Will. He slid forward another foot, Elias' good hand gripping his ankle. Drawing back his arm, he tossed the muffler again.

The scarf brushed the animal's muzzle and he snapped, catching it between his powerful jaws.

"Got him!" Will hauled back on the scarf. "Don't let go of me!"

Will crawled backward, his scarf stretched taut with nearly two-hundred pounds of wet wolf at the other end. The wolf managed to get one back leg and then the other on solid ice. He belly-crawled a few feet before standing erect and shaking the rapidly freezing water from his thick coat.

Now that they had him, Will wondered what they would do with him. The click of the carbine cocking told him Elias wondered, too.

Dropping the scarf end, the wolf took a tentative step toward them.

"No quick moves," hissed Elias.

"No problem," Will whispered anxiously.

Slowly, the boys stepped backward as the wolf advanced. When it reached the pelt, the wolf whimpered, nudging it with his nose, urging her to get up and go with him.

"She's gone," Will said. The wolf looked at him, grey eyes, flecked with gold. Another anxious nuzzle and he bounded away, up the creek bank and into the woods. When it seemed the wolf would melt from sight, he stopped, threw back his head and howled, long and mournfully. When the echo faded, the wolf was gone.

A settling of heavy flakes reminded them of their mission. They'd seen no sign of Jim or of the halfway shack. Snow would soon cover any of Jim's remaining tracks as well as make it difficult for them to find their own trail home. Will dug up his sleeve for his watch. It was almost two o'clock—nearly dusk.

The two headed up the grade and back along their own compacted footsteps toward the main trail and their sled. But the sled was gone, and everything in it.

"Shot must've spooked 'em," said Elias.

"How far do you think they went?"

"Don't know," said Elias. "Could be anywhere by now." Then he sniffed the air and looked puzzled. "Wood smoke." They heard a muffled rifle shot and looked at each other. A signal? Together they followed the sled tracks around the next bend and found their runaway dog team. Blackie had halted it next to the low mound of Jim's halfway shack.

CHAPTER 8

Mounded all around with snow, the log shack looked lower and smaller than Will remembered. In fact, it looked more like a large animal's burrow than shelter for people. Smoke rose from the stovepipe, thin and nearly clear, hardly more than transparent waves of heat.

Except for the smoke, the place looked deserted. Jim's dogsled, pulled up tight by the cabin door, had been snowed on. Jim usually turned his sleds up on the runner ends and leaned them against the eaves. It had been several days since anyone had walked on the path leading to the door. Drifting snow had long since filled the tracks.

Working the hand-carved wooden latch to open the door, the boys entered the windowless cabin, their eyes gradually growing accustomed to the dimness. The Plexiglas skylight, drifted over with snow, admitted only a ghostly blue glow.

Gunpowder fumes hung thick and metallic in the stale air. Will realized why the shot had sounded muffled—Jim had fired from where he lay. Will spotted an eyelet of white light streaming through a new bullet hole in the door.

Jim lay flat on the narrow cot, his rifle on the cot beside him. Empty food tins and wrappers from first-aid supplies lay strewn about. The well-seasoned wood supply, formerly filling almost half the cabin, had been consumed back, nearly out of reach from the cot.

"You made it," Jim murmured. Then grimacing through a spasm of pain, he coughed into a rag.

"Is that blood?" Will exclaimed. "What happened?" His voice squeaked up to an odd note, then cracked mid-word. "What happened," he repeated.

"Fell," Jim whispered. "Followed caribou tracks up a steep hillside." He drew a labored breath. "Snowshoe caught…fell…about thirty feet." He paused to pull another breath.

"We've got to get you out of here," said Will, "there's a storm blowing in from Siberia. Mom's real worried. She's expecting us back by dark."

Jim held up a hand, then let it fall. "Twisted knee. Broken rib. Hard to breathe. Will," he said wearily, "don't know if I can make it back. Go back without me…call for help."

It took a moment to understand what Jim was telling him to do.

He recoiled. "You can forget that. We *are* your help!"

"We're not leaving you," Elias agreed quietly.

Will added up the facts of the situation. Jim had been lying in this cabin too long. A storm like this could last for a week. He knew what they'd find when they returned.

"I'm telling you, go," Jim insisted, half rising then falling back.

"We're going alright," Will assured Jim, "but you're going with us. Will beckoned to Elias, and together they stepped outside, shifting gear to make a space for Jim on the sled.

Elias shouted above the rising wind. "Gonna be tough going."

"Are we wrong? Is he as bad as I think he is? Maybe we ought to hole up here. There's enough food and wood…"

Elias looked at Will, then looked away. His words were soft, but the hard edge of what he said was painfully clear. "I think he goes now or he never goes—while the getting is good."

Will looked around. Already the "getting" didn't look so good.

He eyed his lunch sack longingly. "I'm hungry," he said to Elias. His insides felt like a large empty cave.

"Let's eat later," said Elias, casting an anxious glance at the swirling clouds and gathering darkness. "On the trail."

So, with everything set, Will turned back to the shack to bring Jim out.

He pushed at the door but it didn't budge.

"Must be stuck." But it wasn't stuck.

"Locked us out," said Elias.

"Open up, Jim," Will shouted, pounding the door.

"Get yourselves back to the cabin," Jim groaned. His voice was weak but urgent. "Get out of here!"

"I can't," Will whispered, and slumped against the door. The locked door, along with the idea of the new baby without a father—and himself, for that matter—made Will angry. He kicked the door, then pounded it with his fists. "Open up!" he shouted. "I am not going without you. Please Jim, we're wasting time."

He felt Elias' hand tugging his sleeve. "We can't go without him," Will shouted angrily. Again Elias pulled his sleeve, and Will spun around, ready to vent his frustration on his friend. Elias only jerked his head sideways, toward the top of a tool handle, leaning against the cabin corner, barely showing above the snow. An axe! Bounding through the snow Will seized the handle, and yanked it from where it had frozen in place.

Elias stepped back as Will attacked the door with anger-fueled intensity. Splintering the wooden latch, he sliced each of the three, frozen leather hinges with a single blow. Then, sinking the axe head deeply into the door, he yanked back on it like a door handle, toppling the door completely out of its frame into the snow.

Will was amazed to see Jim standing shakily, weight on his good leg, using a snowshoe as support for the injured one. As Will started for him, Jim held up one hand in a gesture of surrender. "I'll go," he whispered, then grinned painfully. "Before you tear down the rest of my place."

Within minutes they were mushing down the trail. This time it was Jim wrapped in the sleeping bag, tied to the sled.

Will gave him part of a sandwich, but after several bites and a few sips of tea, Jim fell asleep.

Riding the runners briefly while Elias broke trail, Will wolfed a sandwich, pouring tea down the front of his parka, but getting enough in that he felt a little warmer and stronger. "Mush!" he shouted. "Mush!" Then he jumped off the runners, allowing Elias to climb on.

Heading out this morning, the worst of the wind had been behind him. Now, traveling back, they mushed straight into the leading edge of the blizzard. With his hood string knotted short and pulled tightly around his face, his stretched-out muffler over his nose, only his eyes showed. They watered and stung in the blasts of icy wind and particles of snow. Condensation from his breath collected in the muffler, freezing to the beaver-fur ruff of his hood.

The trip had become an endless, mindless drudge of forcing one foot in front of the other. Of pushing the sled and shouting to the dogs. Of taking turns riding or breaking trail, and always keeping on.

The landscape became a gray blur, shot through with whirling, shifting blasts of driven snow. He couldn't see trees beside the trail, couldn't see the trail for that matter. At times Will could scarcely see Blackie at the head of the team.

The storm overtook them in a kind of taunting rhythm. Each gust nearly stopped them in their tracks. They'd falter, then push forward. Push, hold, push, hold. Up the long grade, back across the crusted snow, now frozen thick and hard enough to support their weight.

To Will, trembling with cold and exhaustion, it all mattered less and less. Where he had been cold, he now was growing warmer and he only wanted to sleep. In fact, he'd never wanted to sleep quite so badly. The roar of wind filled his ears and battered him until his brain felt too numb to think. At some point he realized that he'd stopped the sled and stood dozing.

Elias. He looked around for his friend. Sick fear gripped him. Stepping from the runners, he backtracked, counting his paces.

A movement in the mist, darker gray than the storm, became Elias. No longer able to jog, Elias trudged doggedly along, holding his injured arm close to his body.

Will fumbled for a length of harness line from the sled and clumsily knotted a loop around Elias' waist and then around his own. When Will mushed up the team, they traveled no faster than a plod. No more running to keep up. If they didn't make it home soon, they wouldn't.

Without intending to, Will stopped again, and his eyes closed. So sleepy. Maybe they should sit down for just a few minutes. A short nap might help. Just curl up in the snow—how cozy the idea of snuggling into the snow seemed.

Through the din of the storm, Will heard a dog bark. "Go back to sleep, Blackie." Will imagined he was home, snug in his bunk. He slumped over the sled handles.

Another bark pierced his sleepy fog, and another. The sled jerked and started up on its own. He was thrown off-balance by the sudden movement, and nearly fell. Who's driving this team? Will wondered, stumbling behind. He tried to pinch himself awake, but could scarcely feel it through so many layers of clothing.

Walking in his sleep, he tumbled against the sled handles when it stopped. His knees buckled, and he slumped into the snow.

Elias pulled himself along the rope until he caught up with Will. He pulled weakly on the line, urging Will to get up. When Will didn't, Elias plopped down in the snow beside him. The two huddled there, wordless, cold and incredibly sleepy.

In a daze, Will turned his head to see the back of the sled disappear into the snowy gloom. The sigh and moan of the Siberian storm crooned a deadly lullaby. Will had never been so weary in his entire life. "At least I'm warm now," he sighed, and he felt the gentle weight of the snow begin to cover him.

Will dreamed he was swimming. He had dived deep to where the water was warm. But now, regretfully, he was rising through ever-colder water, nearer and nearer the surface. He slowly opened his eyes and found himself being shaken roughly. "Let me sleep! I just wanna sleep," he murmured.

"Will," a familiar voice shouted in his ear. "Willie, wake up."

"Mom?" Will slurred through lips that were too cold to form distinct words. "What are you doing here?"

She pulled him to his feet, then Elias. Snapping a dog lead to the line at Will's waist, she led the boys back along the trail. Will staggered, stumbled and begged to sleep, but mercilessly she dragged them forward. Wrapped in Jim's army parka, the only garment that would close over her, she'd come out with storm lanterns, and hung them by the trail every few hundred yards. She left them now, lit, hanging in the trees, blown nearly sideways by the force of the wind.

Later Mom told them that when the dogs brought the sled in, she had unhitched the team and pulled Jim, sled and all, into the cabin, parking him by the stove. Then, throwing each dog a fish, she grabbed a rifle from the rack, and a fist full of lanterns, and started off in the dark, howling blizzard to find Will.

Will and Elias would only dimly remember a mug of steaming hot cocoa, and being peeled like bananas down to their long johns. Tumbling them into Will's bunk, Mom tucked them beneath her own goose down comforter.

"I'm so proud of you, Willie." There were tears in her eyes as she pulled the blanket to his chin.

Will smiled drowsily, patted her hand and sank into a deep, warm sleep.

"And I was so scared," she whispered as she stroked his sleeping face.

CHAPTER 9

"Fight it," Will moaned. "Don't go to sleep!" But his eyelids refused to stay open. The snow felt so cozy around him, light as feathers and warm as goose down. As he gave himself up to its warmth, an odd thought sifted into his brain. *I am asleep.* His eyes popped open. He lay totally enveloped in his mother's blue goose down quilt, Elias snoring gently beside him.

Comforting sounds drifted from the kitchen. It was the clink-clanking of utensils and the murmur of Mom's voice. He listened for a moment. Had the storm ended? *It's so quiet out,* he thought. *Not just quiet—silent.* Rolling out of his bunk, he crossed to the window and drew back the quilted blinds.

A snowdrift blocked much of his window. From the overhanging eaves, a great cornice of wind-sculpted snow curved smoothly down, insulating and soundproofing the cabin against the arctic blast.

Behind him the door opened. "Oh, you're awake!" His mother came and hugged him. "How do you feel," she asked.

"How do I feel," Will repeated. "Thirsty. I feel like I haven't had a drink in days."

"You haven't."

"I drank tea on the trail yesterday."

"No," she said, "that was the day before yesterday. You slept through yesterday. Oh, you got up once or twice for a few minutes but I don't think you were awake. I know you didn't hear a word I said."

"I slept through yesterday?"

His mother looked at her watch. "You've both been sleeping for thirty-eight hours. I'll bet you're hungry too."

"I could eat a moose!"

Scrounging for his clothes, he suddenly remembered his mission. "How's Jim?"

Her smiled dimmed. "He says he laid there about three days. He didn't have much to eat, and though he melted some snow, I don't think he got enough to drink either. He seems dehydrated." She peered anxiously out the window. "He needs medical attention. How I wish this storm would let up!"

Will thought of his run to the halfway shack. Then his face clouded. "How did Jim..."

"The dogs brought him in," Mom answered his unfinished question. "Come eat and I'll tell you about it."

Jim smiled weakly from a cot near the stove, then closed his eyes and went back to sleep. "I think he's got more color in his face today," Mom said, worry edging her eyes.

CHEECHAKO

Will sipped cocoa while she poured sourdough pancake batter on the sizzling skillet. Elias joined them, yawning. Mom gasped at the sight of his immensely swollen and bruised wrist.

"It's probably just a sprain," Elias murmured, ducking his head shyly.

"It might be broken!"

"Hurts bad enough," he agreed matter-of-factly.

"You want the splint first, or food?"

"Food, please."

As she served up Will's second stack, and he ladled it with wild-blueberry syrup, the lone kerosene lamp flickered and went out.

"Is that it," asked Will, and he shivered, dreading the trip to the kerosene barrel in the barn.

"I'm afraid it is," Mom sighed. "I left the rest of the fuel out along the trail." She glanced at the wood box. "We're also low on firewood, we need supplies from the cache, and the dogs need fed. I've got a few candles. We'll just do without lamps until the storm lets up."

"There's kerosene in the barn, Mom, nearly a full barrel. I can get it."

"No. No way. It's a total whiteout. You can't see more than ten feet in any direction. It's actually kind of eerie—you can't tell the sky from the ground. And the wind's gusting sixty or seventy miles an hour."

"Yeah, but it's just to the barn. Yesterday I..."

"A gust of wind could blow you into the middle of next week. And if you wandered off the trail—it's just not worth it."

"Don't worry," said Elias, reaching for another pancake. "We'd find you in the spring when the drifts melt."

"Oh thanks," said Will.

Mom continued. "I strung a safety line that reaches the cache and woodshed." She pointed at Will. "That's as far as you go. Not to the barn. Understand?"

Will nodded.

"I'll help," said Elias.

"No you won't," Will and his mother replied in unison, and they all laughed. It felt good. There had been little to laugh about lately.

"I'll splint your wrist while Will's doing the chores," Mom added. "Looks like it could use some ice to take down the swelling."

Elias smiled wryly. "Sounds like fun."

They were silent for a moment in the gloom. Will looked over toward Jim. "Is he going to be alright?"

Mom hesitated. "I don't know, Willie, he fell pretty hard. I taped his ribs. I'm pretty sure one of them punctured a lung. His knee is pretty bruised and swollen. Probably tore some ligaments." She raised both hands in a gesture of helplessness and sniffed. Will thought she would cry. But she looked up at him and smiled. "I have my first-aid manual. I'm doing everything I can think of until this darned storm lets up."

"Yeah, but then what?" asked Will as he pulled on his outdoor clothing. "Just because the storm stops doesn't mean the mail plane will come. The Medivac chopper from Fairbanks probably won't just 'happen' to fly over. Jim'll be just as stuck then as he is now."

"We'll worry about that when the storm's over."

Only Will's eyes were visible as he quickly stepped out the cabin door into the wanigan.

His mother's warning followed him. "Don't let go of the line, whatever you do!"

Keeping one hand on the rope was good advice, but not easily followed. Some gusts threatened to blow his feet out from under him. About ten paces from the cabin, leaning nearly diagonally on the wind, Will turned to wave at his mother. She'd be watching his progress through the kitchen window. But the cabin had disappeared.

Can't even see a light. Then he remembered there was no light. At least not enough from the candle to matter. He looked out where the barn would be. *How many thousand times have I walked from here to there?*

Finally the dark square of woodshed appeared out of the gloom. The dogs, lying in the shelter of the shed, leapt up and greeted Will with excited yapping.

"Good dogs!" He returned their greetings with enthusiasm. "Hang on, I'll feed you in a minute. Hey, Blackie girl!" He stopped and scratched her behind both ears before he turned to the woodpile.

Three times, Will made the slow, difficult trek back to the cabin, pulling a sled load of wood. Each time, he saw the relief on his mother's face as he came back through the wanigan door, packing an armload and stomping snow from his mukluks.

Although three sled loads was as much wood as they'd burn in a week, Will returned for a fourth load. He kept thinking about kerosene, and how close the barn really was, even if invisible at the moment.

All the dogsled lines and harnesses hung neatly coiled on the woodshed wall. His mother had strung the longest of the lines to get this far. Will figured he could connect several of the shorter lines to reach the barn. *We could sure use the kerosene.*

Clipping to his mother's safety line, he looked around at the woodshed, the single landmark in this snow-blinded terrain. "Here goes," he sighed, and reeled himself into the swirl, toward the barn, he hoped.

Just as Will reached the end of his rope, and was beginning to worry, the barn floated out of the icy gloom like a schooner on a storm-tossed sea. Somehow he had expected it not to be there. He smiled.

Right. If I can't see it, it isn't there.

As he entered the barn, a blast of wind slammed the door behind him with a violent thwack! The barn had an unaccustomed dry, dusty smell. He could make out the canvas-covered form of their old Farmall tractor, the scent of gasoline mingled with that of old straw and fertilizer. Would summer ever come again?

Enough daydreaming. Will quickly located a two-gallon can and pumped kerosene from the storage barrel. When the can was full, he replaced the bung, and double-checked the lid on the can in his hand.

He braced himself and stepped back out into the jaws of the storm.

Following his make-shift line back to the woodshed, Will wedged the kerosene into the firewood on the sled, then made a quick trip to the nearby cache for a gunnysack full of frozen food for both people and dogs.

"Okay, guys, it's chow!" Will hollered to the dogs as he pulled dried fish out of the sack. "Ho, ho, ho! Have you been good little dogs this year? Yes? Then Santa has something for you." Will tossed a fish to each waiting dog, then unsnapped Blackie's line. "Come on, girl. You want to go with me?"

She definitely did.

Will pulled the sled, loaded with supplies into the wanigan, and scarcely got the outer door fastened behind himself and Blackie before his mother popped out the inner door.

"Will, what took you so long? I..." She saw the kerosene can and stopped. "Oh Will, what am I going to do with you?"

He grinned sheepishly. "You could ground me."

"Good idea," she agreed. "You're grounded."

"Ah, Mom! Elias and I were just going to the movies!"

Mom laughed and ruffled his hair. "Do you miss Boston and your other life too terribly, honey?"

"Sometimes," Will replied. "City life is a lot easier." Then he grinned. "But it's not as exciting."

Together they refilled the lanterns and lit, not just one, but three.

"Go for it, Mom!" Will teased. "Get wild and crazy!"

That day, Will caught her looking at him thoughtfully— a different kind of look. He didn't know how a look could make a guy feel more grown-up, but this one did.

CHAPTER 10

Will sat bolt upright in his bunk. Fumbling in darkness for his flashlight, he checked his watch. Five o'clock. Then he slipped from beneath his toasty comforter and tiptoed to the window. It was so cold, he could see his own breath. A layer of ice glazed the inside of the window. Will melted a spot with his thumb to read the thermometer outside. Ten degrees below zero.

He heard a rustling from the bunk.

"What time is it," murmured Elias, half asleep. "What are you doing?"

"It's early," Will whispered. "The storm has stopped and I'm going for help."

"I'm going, too," said Elias, throwing back the covers. The sudden movement made him wince.

"Your arm's busted, you can't come. Besides, even with a broken arm, Mom and Jim need you here.

"But..." said Elias.

"You know I'm right."

"Yeah," Elias agreed reluctantly. "Will you let my folks know I'm okay?"

"Sure. Boy do I wish you could come."

"Your folks aren't going to like this."

"They won't know 'til I'm gone. You can tell them which way I went after I leave. I'm taking the main trail to Nenana. How hard can that be?"

"When the storm's over," Mom had said, "we'll stamp out a distress signal in the snow, or something. Planes are bound to fly over."

But Will had his doubts. Jim grew weaker by the hour. *So I guess it's up to me*, he decided, and began to dress for the trip.

Into a knapsack he threw waterproof matches, tea bags, honey, biscuits, candy bars and moose jerky. Not much, but enough to keep him going for a day or two. "If I'm still out there after that," Will thought grimly, "I'll be too dead to eat, anyway."

Last night, when he'd gone out to 'check on the dogs,' he'd packed everything he would need on the small sled.

"You crazy cheechako," whispered Elias as Will silently eased himself out the door.

"You've got part of that right," Will whispered back.

"What? Crazy or cheechako?"

CHEECHAKO

"We'll find out in a couple of days." Will smiled and closed the door quietly behind him, Blackie at his heels.

The fierce wind had gone, but the drifts in the yard stood chest high in places. The sled dogs were sleeping snug and warm, completely covered by soft snow.

Will decided to run only five dogs. That would leave enough for Elias to put together a team if he had to.

Snapping the last dog into harness he straightened, noticing that the sky was clear and ablaze with stars. Cautiously, he slipped the tether, grabbed the sled handles and stepped to the runners. "Mush," he called softly. "Mush!" Ready to run, the dogs bounded eagerly, picking up the trail even through the drifted snow.

By this time tomorrow, help would be on its way. "All I've got to do is to make it to Nenana," Will told himself firmly. First, he would navigate the drifted trail along a portion of an abandoned trap line. That would intersect with another section of the old Mail Trail. Where the trail crossed the Tanana he would finally meet the highway. If he could manage to flag down a car, he could ask them to send help. Someone would summon the military helicopter from Fairbanks.

A few miles out, the trail led behind a hill and into the trees. Drifts gave way to about six inches of snow over hard-pack. After all they'd been through, this was easy going. Will divided his time between riding the runners and jogging behind. At first, he felt stiff and a little sore. But soon he felt like he could run all day, which was good, because he probably would.

The rigors of these last few months—even the last few days—had changed Will. He felt lean and tough, trail-ready. That thought led to another, which made him laugh. *Now I'm almost as tough as my mother. I wouldn't be here if she hadn't come out after me.* Pound for pound, she still had more guts than anybody he knew.

Just at dawn, he pulled up the dogs and stepped on the brake. "Whoa!" The team stopped willingly, lapping mouthfuls of powdery snow with long, thirsty tongues. Puffs of their breath turned to gold in the rising sun.

Will tied the sled securely to a sapling, and pulled out kindling to start a small fire. Melting snow, he brewed strong tea and laced it with honey, like he'd seen the seasoned mushers do. The hot tea and honey—and the chance to rest—refreshed him.

Crouching by his fire, he searched the clear sky for aircraft he could signal, anything to speed up the rescue, but saw nothing.

Downing the last of his tea he kicked snow on the fire and gripped the handles of the sled. "Hi you, mush!" he shouted to the huskies. They yipped and broke into that steady trot sled dogs can maintain for miles. *So far, so good*, thought Will.

About an hour later he began recognizing landmarks that meant he was near the old slide area, an unstable section of hillside where Jim had narrowly missed being taken out by an avalanche. Two trails met here, and two valleys. Will would travel nearly ten miles to get around this hill. The trail he needed lay just on the other side.

CHEECHAKO

Will's spirits rose when he saw the trail break out of the trees into the open. He whistled and shouted to the dogs, who sensed his excitement.

But as they emerged from the trees, those same spirits took a flaming nose-dive.

The trail intersection had completely disappeared.

A massive avalanche, more than a mile long, by the look of it, had buried the trail, the landmarks and had even changed the contour of the land. Over that, several feet of fresh snow had blown and drifted, rippling like ocean waves across the jumbled landscape.

Some of the drifts stood more than five feet high. "The dogs will never get through this," he groaned, frustrated beyond endurance.

Feeling discouraged and cranky, Will fumbled in the pack for his snowshoes.

Slogging through deep drifts, he broke trail for the team. Twice Blackie, following too closely, stepped on the back of Will's snowshoe, throwing him on his face into the snow.

Soon Will was sweating with exertion, angry at himself, at Blackie, at the storm and the slide. He was even angry at Jim for getting himself injured.

When they stopped to rest, Will noticed how 'warm' the air had become, probably twenty degrees above zero. Above them, on the steep face of the hill, the increased weight of all that melting snow could easily cause another avalanche.

The knot of anger in his belly turned to fear that kept him looking anxiously up the slope. He forced himself to pick up speed and hold the pace to get past the slide. But even as he tugged the lead line, urging the team forward, he felt, as well as heard, a hollow, echoing rumble directly above them.

It seemed the entire hillside was rushing down to swallow them. It would reach them in seconds.

Will scrambled to unclip the team from the sled. "Go, go!" he screamed in panic.

Terrified by the rumble and shaking of the earth, the dogs tried to bolt into the trees, but something brought them up short. Blackie! Dragged by the team, her lead line had snagged tight on a birch.

Will grabbed the hatchet from where he'd tucked it on the sled. It would be her only chance. He tensed, focused and threw it with all his strength. The hatchet spun once, twice, then ker-thunk!

The impact of the slide lifted Will and the sled off the ground, ripping his snowshoes off his feet and tossing them willy-nilly. One moment he was struggling to remain upright, the next he was buried, desperately clawing for the surface.

Jim had told him about snow slides. "You have to swim in the wave of snow as it sweeps along. Swim to the surface," he said. "Because when the snow finally stops, it settles quickly, becoming so heavy, it's impossible to move, or dig out."

Abruptly, the snow churning around Will's helpless body stopped. He had just seconds before the soft snow settled and he'd be trapped forever.

Frantically, Will cupped his hands around his face, to create an air pocket. Otherwise, he might suffocate before he could be rescued.

Rescued? He laughed to himself bitterly. I was supposed to *be* the rescue. Mom and Jim and Elias were counting on me. Just look at me now!

CHAPTER 11

I'm buried alive!

The weight of the snow held Will motionless, helpless. Fear made him nearly sick to his stomach. He wanted to scream and cry, but he couldn't afford to waste the air.

A dim, blue light filtered through from above. How far to the surface?

Blackie. Where was she? Had the hatchet cut the harness line? Did she scramble to safety or was she buried just as deeply and permanently as Will. The thought of Blackie trapped, struggling, made his eyes sting and tears well up—tears he couldn't even reach to wipe away.

He tried to move, to dig. Jim was right. It was impossible. Without wanting to, he began to think about what would happen. He could only take shallow breaths, and the more he tried to breathe, the more difficult it became. Soon he'd run out of air, and just go to sleep. And that would be it. Maybe they'd find him in the spring, or maybe an animal would...

CHEECHAKO

Will heard a scratching, snuffing sound. Digging? *I'm found!* His heart pounded with relief. He tried to shout. "I'm here!"

But he quickly realized that he wasn't found. There wouldn't be any people way out here. Nobody saw the slide, so nobody knows where I am. A fresh wave of panic swept over him.

A bear? He imagined a grizzly digging him up for breakfast. No, it couldn't be a bear in the middle of winter. They're hibernating. And yet, something was digging.

The sound grew closer, and the blue light shone brighter. Suddenly a shaft of daylight burst through, and a rush of sweet fresh air. He filled his aching lungs and gathered himself to face the snuffing carnivore. But the snuffing carnivore stopped digging and licked Will's ear.

"Blackie!" he shouted, laughing and crying at the same time. "You good dog." In minutes, with the help of Blackie's frenzied digging, Will worked his arms loose and dug himself out of his snowy grave.

He knelt by the spunky lead dog and hugged her hard. She wriggled with happiness.

The sled, jammed against a tree, had smashed nearly in half. And, with the exception of Blackie, the dogs were gone. Surveying the huge slide area, he searched in vain for some sign of them.

As he turned his attention to salvaging supplies for the trip, his body shook with sobs, and tears streamed down his cheeks. Will said an awkward prayer for his missing dogs. He wasn't sure who would hear his prayer—or if it was even okay to pray for dogs. But to Will, they had become less like working dogs and more like companions and friends.

His pack was skewed, but still tied to the busted sled, still filled with provisions, his sleeping bag, and flashlight. One snowshoe remained unbroken and the other he repaired with a branch.

Will weighed his alternatives. He could head back to the cabin, having wrecked the sled, lost the team, and accomplished nothing. Or he could walk, maybe another twenty or thirty hours, following the trail along the winding frozen river.

There was one other possibility. He could go straight up over the top of this hill and hope to come down near the highway on the other side, cutting the distance in half.

The prospect of leaving the trail made him uneasy. "I'll just have to risk it," he decided, and started up the slope.

Several hours later, just at the top of an outcrop, the last of the daylight left him, but not before he saw the flag.

Tied to the branch of a leafless cottonwood, hung a fragment of weathered red flannel. In the fading light, Will spotted a blaze on a tree farther up—a marked tree. "A trail. I've found a trail." It helped to know he wasn't the first person to attempt this shortcut.

From where he stood at last light, he could make out the entire layout of the trail, winding up and around the face of the summit.

CHEECHAKO

Freshly elated, he turned to look out across the flats, searching for the soft yellow glow of a window full of kerosene lamplight. But from this distance he saw nothing. Feeling empty and lonely, Will resumed his climb just to put those wretched feelings behind him.

Hours later, having crossed the summit by moonlight and flashlight, he crawled into his bedroll, nestled in soft, dry powdery snow. Chewing a strip of moose jerky, he tossed a dried fish to Blackie, who curled up beside him. Closing his eyes he slept instantly, awakening once when a wolf howled in the distance. Blackie growled low in her throat but Will had already sunk back into a dreamless sleep.

Fresh snow fell, tickling Will's nose, awakening him. Blackie licked his face and tried to climb into the bag with him. Gently pushing her off, he climbed out, shivering. "No time for a fire, girl," he said, "we'll have to hit the trail and warm up walking."

Will thought that once he crossed the summit, he might recognize a landmark. But in the snow and ice fog he could scarcely see a thing. "At least we're headed downhill," he sighed, not very encouraged.

His legs ached, his back ached and he was cold, although he had stopped shivering. He ate a couple of biscuits and a candy bar as he walked, which raised his spirits a little.

Will's relief at heading downhill was short-lived. He descended from a cloud, and haze of lightly falling snow into a shallow valley. With about a quarter-mile of visibility, he made out the trail rising again, up another hill. He wanted to sit down right there and wait for spring.

Blackie growled, a low menacing warning. Ears tipped forward, her nose tested the air, and the hair along her neck and the ridge of her back bristled. Will heard the sound, and dived behind a small drift, pulling Blackie down close in the snow. Loping from the ice fog and falling snow, yipping excitedly, came a wolf pack, hunting. He and Blackie were upwind, so the wolves probably hadn't seen them—yet.

Then Will spotted their quarry. The pack was trying to bring down an adult moose. He knew that wolves usually try to single out a very young, very old, or injured animal. This moose appeared to be young and strong, with no inclination to be wolf chow. Will guessed the wolves must be very hungry and had chosen badly.

Spinning quickly, the moose lowered his rack—at least four feet from tip-to-tip—and scooped a wolf clear off the ground, tossing him end-over-end into a drift. As others tried to attack from the rear, the moose rocked forward on his front legs, lashing out with both back legs, sending a pair of wolves rolling and yelping.

After a few minutes, the wolves limped away, licking their wounds and probably looking for smaller game. *Like us,* thought Will. He whispered to Blackie, "Let's get out of here." Suddenly the uphill trail looked more inviting.

The light snow gradually became dense and wind-driven, and it occurred to Will that maybe he'd miscalculated. The blizzard had not blown over. He guessed the hours of clear sky had been the 'eye' at the center of the storm, like the hole in a doughnut.

CHEECHAKO

Although Will had started leading Blackie, at some point he realized that Blackie now led him. When he could no longer tell if he was even on the trail, he tied the harness line around his wrist and let her pull and guide him through endless drifts.

Whether they had walked one hour or ten, Will could not be sure. But after they slid to the bottom of a sudden steep incline, Blackie stopped and would go no farther.

Will's hopes, which had been revived by his lead dog's determination, now fell. "Come on, Blackie," he encouraged, "just a little more."

She refused to budge. He begged and pleaded. He shouted angrily. Finally he cuffed the dog along the side of her head. He doubted it hurt her through the thick moose hide mitt, but it hurt her feelings, and she slunk down in the snow. Ashamed to tears, Will knelt and put his arms around her. She quickly forgave him and licked his muffler where his cheek would have been.

He tried to pick her up and carry her, but she wriggled away. "I'm not leaving you," said Will. With a shock he realized this meant they had come to the end of the trail.

Somewhere in another world, his mother, Jim and Elias were waiting out the storm. He knew his parents were worried sick about his foolish attempt to get help. And it looked like they had cause to be. He'd gone and got himself lost in a stupid blizzard.

He patted Blackie's head, knowing he should leave her if she refused to come. Blackie was just a dog, after all. But he'd saved her life, and she'd saved his—twice.

"Anyway, I'm dead even if I try to go on without you," he told the dog. "I have no idea where we are. We'll hole up and wait this thing out. We'll be okay, you'll see."

But he didn't believe it anymore. He believed they would die here. Just the same, Will settled down beside his dog and began to unpack his bedroll.

Abruptly the noise of the storm increased in its intensity, although Will didn't think the snow was falling any harder. The wind actually seemed to have eased up. Yet, strangely the rumble increased to an alarming roar.

Suddenly, the semi-darkness was suffused with brilliant yellow and flashing-orange light. A deafening blast of the snowplow's air horn battered Will and set Blackie off in a frenzy of frightened barking. He jumped to his feet but his knees buckled, and he sat back down hard in the snow.

As the huge truck shuddered to a halt, the driver's door swung wide and their rescuer jumped down from the cab and came running toward them. Will threw his arms around Blackie's neck and fought back tears. "You good dog," he shouted. "You saved us!"

Blackie had stopped and planted them in the middle of the snow-drifted highway.

CHAPTER 12

"I'm Len," said the snowplow operator, urging the huge machine into motion, "and you're...?"

"Will. Will Rollins."

"You're lucky I spotted you, Will," he said. "Another few seconds and..." He hesitated but Will understood. He'd seen the front blade, with its huge disks gnashing and devouring the snow, then spitting it into a neat snow bank by the side of the road. Will shuddered.

"What are you doing all the way out here, kid? Where do you live, and where are your folks?"

So, Will told him. And he hadn't spoken more than a few words before Len grabbed his radio microphone. He called in a message to the state highway garage at Nenana, less than five miles away.

"Yes, I'm sure it's an emergency, Vera," he growled at the dispatcher. "Scramble the M.A.S.T. unit at Fort Wainwright...just as soon as the weather opens up."

111

The snowplow finally reached Nenana, and rumbled up the wide main street. Len plowed up a side street, nearly burying cars, pickups and snowmobiles which were already solidly drifted into place.

"We're headed for the school, aren't we?" asked Will. They rounded the corner and there was Nenana Public School looking much as he'd left it, except for five or six extra feet of snow—seven or eight feet in some of the taller drifts. "I've never seen so much snow!"

Len grinned. "They're calling this one of the storms of the century. Wouldn't you know it would arrive on the day you decide to walk to town. This one's big even for Alaska."

They turned off the street onto what was normally a parking lot. Without stopping, they plowed through the lot and onto the baseball field. Reaching the far side, Len swept the plow in a circle, scraping most of the infield clear in minutes.

When Len turned the key off, the silence was nearly as deafening as its roar. Will's ears rang with the sudden change.

"Vera says you're to wait at the school," Len said. "Can you make it in by yourself?"

"Sure," Will replied. "Now that I'm thawed, I'm almost good as new."

"What would it take to make you good as new?" Len wanted to know.

"Food! I could eat a moose."

"We'll see what we can scrounge up. Fresh out of moose, though," Len added with a chuckle.

Will went into the school building where school kids on spring break sat watching *The Three Stooges* being projected on the wall. Mrs. Freeman, the teacher, brought a cup of hot chocolate for Will and a bowl of warm canned milk for Blackie.

While Len went to the Coffee Cup Café to get food, Will called Elias' folks. At the news that her son was safe, Elias' mom couldn't speak. Instead she let out a little sob and handed the phone to her husband. "His mother was starting to get worried," Mr. Charlie said. There was a long pause. "Me too."

Soon Len returned with the best-smelling burger and fries of Will's life. Hot food never tasted so good. He finished off with a huge piece of cherry pie, downing the meal in way fewer bites than his mother would have approved. Then he stretched out on the carpet beside Blackie. "We made it," Will grinned as he patted her head and yawned.

In what seemed like moments, Len's voice woke him. "Come on Will, wake up. Storm's over. It's morning."

"Morning?" Will looked at his watch. He felt like he'd only just closed his eyes. Someone had covered him with a parka. He struggled stiffly to his feet and into his gear. If there was a part of him that wasn't sore, he couldn't find it.

First, Will heard the percussive impact of helicopter blades—wok, wok, wok, wok. Then a huge, olive-drab Huey chopper, shaped like a giant banana, approached the cleared landing area. Soldiers in arctic survival gear jumped to the ground before the craft had even settled. Len, trailed by Will and Blackie, rushed out the school's double doors to meet them.

One of the soldiers, a black man identified by his I.D. plate as Lieutenant S. Harlan, jogged neatly to the group.

Len stepped up to shake the lieutenant's hand, then beckoned to Will. Shouting to make himself heard over the ticking, roaring whine of the idling helicopter, Len said "Will, this is Lieutenant Harlan."

"Call me Steve," said the lieutenant, shaking Will's hand. "Now what's this about your parents?"

Will told him about Jim's injury. "We've got to hurry," Will said, with a renewed sense of urgency.

Steve put a reassuring hand on Will's shoulder. "Don't worry, we'll do everything we can to get to them, but..." he hesitated, "how did you get here?"

Len laughed. "By dogsled," he volunteered. "And on foot."

The lieutenant's eyebrows raised. "Tough kid. That's no small distance. You did good. Now, are you ready to go back?"

"Yes, but…" stammered Will. "I can't leave Blackie."

"Bring her," Steve said. He pointed to the pink rim of dawn, lining the horizon. "But let's get going. We have an opening."

Happily, Will, with Blackie close at his heels, jogged along behind Steve's long strides to the helicopter. Steve bounded up the three-step ladder, turning with hands out. "Hand me the dog," he shouted. Will grabbed Blackie and, just as he handed her up, someone snapped a photograph. The brilliant blue-white flash startled Will, temporarily blinding him.

By the time Will felt his way up the ladder and into the belly of the chopper, Blackie stood tethered, about half-way back the main cabin, next to a fold-down jump seat that Steve indicated for him. Strapped flat to stretchers, two other uniformed men waved, then went back to napping.

"They have to sleep when they can," explained Steve. "They may be up all night."

Behind him, the heavy door chunked shut, and instantly the chopper rose.

Staggering slightly, Will dropped into his seat, quickly buckling himself in while the schoolyard, Len waving, and even the mighty snowplow fell away and became tiny.

Nose pressed to the scratched, high-impact plastic window, Will watched as Nenana became a checkerboard of log cabins, shacks, and sheds. At the many doghouses, the shaggy inhabitants were out, noses to the sky, barking up a frenzy.

The helicopter whirled, side-slipped and dropped a bit, leaving Will's stomach to catch up on its own.

A motion from Steve caught his eye. He pantomimed putting on the headphones that Will found hanging at his elbow. Nothing like the headphones for his portable tape recorder, these were sturdy and hard-shelled. In fact, Will felt like he was wearing a well-padded turtle on each ear.

"Is this a microphone, too," he asked. The sound of his own voice in his ears made Steve's nod unnecessary.

As the helicopter turned south, following the frozen river, Lieutenant Harlan questioned Will on details of finding their cabin from the air.

"How many miles would you guess?

"My dad says between fifteen and twenty."

"East or west of the river?"

"West bank, set back about two-hundred feet in a clearing."

"How many outbuildings?"

"Three. Well, four, counting the wood shed."

"Any other landmarks?"

"Yeah. The property sits on a bend in the river. I've never seen it from the air, but I think it would be easy to spot. I hope they're not too mad at me for taking off without telling them."

"That was a pretty dumb thing to do," Steve agreed solemnly.

"I know, but I didn't know what else to do," he said. "I guess I should have talked to Mom, though…"

"You're right," agreed the voice in his ears. They're probably worried sick. Leaving an injured man and a pregnant

116

woman—without even telling them your plans—that's about the most immature, reckless, foolhardy...brave act I've heard of."

Will chewed his lip anxiously.

"On the other hand," Steve continued, "if you hadn't gone for help, we wouldn't be..." He looked at his watch. "...about five minutes from rescue right now. It could have been days or weeks before help came flying by. From the sound of it, that might have been too late."

Steve pointed out the portside window. "Is that it?"

"Yes! That's it. That's our place," Will shouted. Steve flinched. "Oops, sorry." Will lowered his voice to a more comfortable level for the sensitive headphones.

"Do me a favor and give those soldiers a tap," Steve said into Will's headset.

He did, and they woke instantly, sat up, and pulled on boots and military-issue parkas over their insulated jumpsuits.

The cabin and all the outbuildings, except the cache, were mostly buried on their south walls, with snow drifted over the roofs. The cache looked as though Will could walk right to the door on the snow. He couldn't see the ladder from where he sat.

"No smoke," muttered Steve's electrical voice in Will's ear. "I don't like the looks of that."

Will started to say 'Jim builds a smokeless fire,' but the words stuck in his throat. If there were a fire in that stove, it was not only smokeless, but heatless. Will could tell from drifting snow around the chimney that there had been no fire—at least since yesterday.

Slowly, agonizingly slowly it seemed to Will, the chopper approached the cabin, aiming for the snow shadow on the north side.

Hurry, hurry. Will leaned into his seat belt. The trip flying out now seemed much shorter than this dawdling landing.

As Will felt the helicopter skis settle into the snow, he snapped loose his seat belt and jumped to his feet. He prepared to follow the two medics, who were already slogging through thigh-deep snow, carrying a wire stretcher between them. Poised in the door, ready to jump, Will felt a strong hand on his arm.

"Wait," said Steve's voice in his earphones. It sounded suspiciously like a command.

"Why?" Will protested.

"For one thing," the lieutenant explained, "you're still wearing your headset."

"For another," Steve continued, "my men need the opportunity to get into the cabin and assess the situation medically without you in the way."

Will nodded, impatiently, hating the suspense of waiting behind. Minutes ticked by—nearly forty-five of them—and still no word. *What could be wrong? What could be taking so long?* Will began to fear the worst.

A sudden rattle of headphone static made his breath catch in his throat.

"Situation stable here, Lieutenant," reported a medic from inside the cabin. Will heard a click, more static and an odd, wailing kind of interference.

"Affirmative, Sergeant," Steve responded with obvious relief.

"Lieutenant?"

"Here," said Steve.

"We'll need that second stretcher." Will raised his eyes to Steve's. The voice continued, "Why don't you send it in with the boy."

They heard more static, more weird radio interference, and a click as the circuit closed.

Will peeled off his headset, wondering just how bad it was going to be in the cabin.

Maybe they just don't want to give me bad news over the radio, Will thought, his hands trembling so that he had trouble pulling on his mitts.

But when Will looked up, Lieutenant Harlan was smiling. He grabbed Will's arm. "Hey, don't you get it? They're okay!"

"But if they're okay, why did it take so long? Why do they need a second stretcher?" Will protested.

Steve shrugged an exaggerated I-don't-know gesture. "Why don't you go find out?"

Will jumped into the snow, and Steve handed him the rescue basket.

A medic met him in the wanigan, taking the stretcher, knocking the snow off, then carrying it inside. As he went back in, he left the door open. Something inside Will objected. He and his folks were always careful to conserve heat. Then he realized that it was probably the same temperature inside as it was outside.

"Why didn't Elias keep the fire going—or Mom," he wondered, looking around the wanigan. It was still half-filled with firewood.

Jim lay strapped to the stretcher in the kitchen. Still wrapped in his down sleeping bag, not much more than his eyes showed, but they were open and looking at Will with relief and joy.

"Thank God!" he whispered weakly. "And thank *you*! You saved us. But Will," Jim smiled a little. "One of these days, we need to talk about..."

"I know," Will interrupted. "I'm sorry I didn't tell you and Mom I was going, but I was pretty sure you wouldn't allow it."

"You were right."

"You men can work this out later," said the medic briskly. "We need to be moving out of here." They grabbed the stretcher between them and were out the door.

Elias, also wrapped in a down bag, welcomed his friend with a broad grin. "Well, I guess now we know which it is."

"Which is what?" Will asked, puzzled.

"You're not a cheechako, but you *are* crazy!"

Will heard his mother calling from her bedroom. His knees went weak with relief. He didn't even care if she chewed him out for pulling such a stupid stunt. She was okay!

"Will, come in here!" Mom lay on the stretcher, pale and exhausted-looking, waiting her turn to be transported to the chopper.

"Mom! What's wrong? What happened?"

"Oh Willie," was all she could say when she saw him. Tears rolled freely down her cheeks.

"I'm sorry, Mom, don't cry," he exclaimed. "You were okay when I left. What happened?"

"Will," said one of the medics. "Hold this."

Distracted, Will turned to help the medic, who handed him a bundle. But instead of first aid supplies or medical instruments, the bundle began to wriggle and wail. Now Will knew why Steve had been grinning. That wasn't interference in the radio signal, it was a baby crying.

Smiling, tears still in her eyes, Mom spoke over the indignant protests of the tiny new creature.

"This is your sister. Will, meet Amanda."

CHAPTER 13

Will throttled back the outboard motor, expertly sliding the long freight boat bow onto the packed-sand riverbank at Nenana. In a single move he cut the ignition as he tipped up and locked the outboard motor, to keep the propeller blades from fouling in the sand.

Deftly Will climbed over the boat's payload to leap dry-footed from the bow. He made the line fast to an exposed stub of galvanized pipe, pounded deep into the riverbank.

Straightening, he turned to study the Tanana River on this cool sunny morning in early July. Silty brown, whirlpooled and swirled, the Tanana flowed swiftly again. How vividly he remembered its stillness and frozen grandeur as the helicopter had lifted off, carrying his family and his friend away. Left by himself, it would be his job to feed the dogs and watch the homestead until their return.

At first Will thought he might be lonely by himself. But chores kept him busy, and Blackie was good company. In a couple of weeks the first pools of melt-water had appeared on the snow of the frozen river. Then, in a single day, the entire sheet of river ice swept downstream, and Will knew summer would sweep in behind just as quickly.

Within a few days of break-up, the echoing whine of an outboard motor told him his alone days were over. The family, including baby Amanda, was finally home. That evening, Will couldn't stop smiling, he was so glad to see them. And he couldn't help having seconds and thirds of the first good meal he'd had in more than a month.

Now standing on the summer-washed bank of the Tanana, last winter seemed like another life, another world. Whistling for Blackie, Will turned toward town. How different it looked today with the stands of birch and cottonwood leafed out green, and the high expanse of black-steel railroad bridge silhouetted against the flawless blue Alaska sky.

Ahead on his right stood the railroad station and the riverfront docks where he'd first seen—and resued—Blackie. As Will watched, a huge rusty crane off-loaded pallets of machinery from flatcars.

Bending to stroke Blackie's sleek head, Will caught a movement out of the corner of his eye.

It was Daniel Silas, an Athabascan boy Will knew slightly from his time at the Nenana school. Will nodded a cautious greeting.

"Your boat?" asked Daniel.

"Belongs to my family."

"Nice landing."

"Thanks," said Will, searching the other's face for possible trouble, and finding none.

"Is this Blackie?" Daniel asked.

"Yeah."

"Okay to pet her?"

"Sure," said Will. "How do you know Blackie?"

"I just heard around." Daniel bent to scratch Blackie behind the ears. "Not many lead dogs like this one." Blackie, sensing praise, raised a cloud of fine river silt with her thumping tail.

He must be okay, thought Will, relaxing a little. *Blackie likes him.*

Without saying much, the boys and Blackie walked up and over the tracks toward the depot.

At the depot, Jim stepped down from the running board of a borrowed pickup, his limp only slightly noticeable. "Any problems with the boat?" he asked.

Will grinned. "No, it was easy."

"I saw him land," said Daniel. "Looked like he was born on the river." He turned to Will. "You gonna be uptown later?"

"Yeah—soon as we unload this stuff at the store."

"See you there."

"Looks like you made another friend," said Jim as Will watched Daniel walk away.

"Looks like it," said Will. "Usually people here only see me doing something stupid—like charging out onto break-up ice to save a dog. Or getting caught out in a blizzard. I have to admit it's nice to have somebody catch me doing something right for a change."

"Son, you have more courage and natural gumption than you give yourself credit for. It's something you either have or you don't. That kind of thing can't be learned. And you've got it."

"You think so, Jim?"

"Yep."

"Chip off the old block, right?

They grinned at each other. Will had never been happier.

But as they unloaded their produce, he felt a growing sense of unease at the prospect of facing everybody again. "Maybe I'll just stay here by the boat," he said, though he loved his trips to Coghill's. Jim had promised him a pair of summer sneakers next time they were in town. By July his work boots felt like hot iron on his feet.

From somewhere over the tracks, he heard an explosive sound like a truck backfiring, then another and another. He looked at Jim quizzically. "Sounds like shots," he said, but then couldn't imagine who would be firing a gun right in the middle of town—even in Alaska.

Jim grinned. "Not shots," he said, and dug in his shirt pocket. "Fireworks." He pulled out two small brightly-colored packages. Tossing one to Will, he quickly lit the other, flinging it up the deserted beach to blow itself to pieces in an exploding rampage of sparkle and din. "Happy Fourth of July!" he shouted. For a moment Will stood, speechless at the sight of Jim, normally reserved, cutting loose.

"I forgot it was the Fourth of July. I forgot about fireworks and parades. I forgot about holidays, period."

Jim laughed. "That's how it gets when you live in the woods all the time. You'll like an Alaskan holiday. After the long, cold snowbound winters, any excuse to celebrate will do. They once had a parade right up Main Street—pickup trucks and bicycles with crepe paper streamers—for a guy that won a big poker hand at Moocher's Bar."

Will fingered his firecrackers. "I think I'll save mine for later." He hoped Elias was in town. It wouldn't be much of a celebration without a friend to set them off with.

The truck loaded, they headed back across the tracks toward the general store. Nenana's main street had been blocked for races and games. It looked to Will like the whole town had turned out for the fun.

While Jim was settling up with Coghill, Will wandered through the warehouse and into the back of the store. Grandma Coghill, folding and shelving work pants, noticed him coming through the back, and turned.

"You can't bring your dog into the store," she said in her quavery voice. Then she looked at him more closely across the top of her wire-rim glasses. "Oh, it's you, Will. I didn't recognize you." She stopped folding pants and bent to pet the dog. "Come on ahead this time," she said. "I didn't realize this was Blackie. Can I help you find something?"

"I was hoping to find some sneakers."

She dropped her gaze to his hot, booted feet.

"I'll just bet you are," she said. "Follow me." She led Will around the hunting-knife display case and through a door into the old store, which was Coghill's original store from the 1920s. Dimly lit, with just a few shadeless light bulbs hung high, the whole place held an air of magic for Will.

They passed bundles of bear-paw snowshoes hanging on the wall. They threaded down narrow aisles between beaver traps and kerosene lanterns, a rack of shovels and rakes, a small dogsled, several brand-new fat-tired bicycles, and shelves and shelves of soft goods. The air held a timeless perfume—decades of scents of leather, liniment, tar, rubber, mothballs, and gun oil.

Picking their way around and through, they ended up at the front of the old store, just inside the display windows which had been mostly painted over. There, a single row of ancient theater seats faced the street, and Grandma Coghill motioned Will toward them.

She stared at Will's feet with her practiced eye. She'd been putting shoes on Nenana feet for more than fifty years.

"Size seven-and-a-half," she guessed correctly. Turning, she grabbed a tall ladder, which rolled along the shelf-front on a track. Once up the ladder, she pulled herself along with a practiced hand, rummaging the racked, red boxes at the top. Watching, Will pushed one of the seats flat and sat.

From his vantage in the darkened store, Will peered out onto the sunny street where the people of Nenana, young and old, celebrated Independence Day. Daniel and some of his friends were laughing and thumping each other at the dart-throwing booth. *Looks like fun,* Will thought wistfully.

Blackie selected a spot on the wood-planked floor near Will. Settling her chin on crossed paws, she watched with ears forward as Grandma Coghill deftly laced the sneakers on Will's feet.

Standing on a square of old carpet, Will bounced and twisted his feet to test the fit.

"These are nice," he said, but his voice had an empty sound, even to him.

The old lady looked at him sharply. Cocking her head she regarded him over her glasses. "You don't sound like they're all that nice." She moved to climb back up the ladder. "Would you like me to see if I can find another color?"

Then she followed Will's gaze to the boys in the street. For a long moment the two stood, silent. Glittering dust motes drifted in a single beam of sunlight that pierced the gloom. "I remember the first time you came in here," she said.

Uh-oh, thought Will. Nearing eighty-five, Grandma Coghill was known for remembering the first time some of his schoolmates' grandparents had come into the store.

CHEECHAKO

"You were six inches shorter, pudgy, and you didn't want to be here. Do you remember what you said to me?"

Will couldn't remember his first time in the store, let alone anything he'd said. "I—I don't remember," he stammered.

"You said you didn't like anybody here and you wanted to go back to Boston."

"I said that?"

"I'll bet today there isn't any place you'd rather be than Alaska—am I right?"

"You're right," said Will, the realization washing over him.

"You're not a cheechako any more."

She looked down at Will's new sneakers and picked up his work boots. "I'll put these boots with the rest of your dad's gear in back." She dug deep in an apron pocket and pulled out a quarter. "Here, this is a loan. It costs a quarter to enter a race, and you look pretty fast in those new tennies, so I'll stake you. You get on out in the street and give those boys a run for their money."

Will stepped out onto the wood-planked sidewalk in front of the store, squinting a little. On his right, a huge banner stretched the full width of the street. "Starting line," he read. "She's right, I feel fast!"

A newspaper article, neatly cut and taped inside the store window, caught Will's eye. "Dogsled Rescue," he read aloud. "'Nenana Boy Mushes to Save Family in Blizzard.'

"That's us!" There was the photograph of himself with Blackie in his arms, climbing into the helicopter.

"Will..." a familiar voice called. Elias jogged toward him, trailed by Daniel and a group of other boys Will recognized from school—including Edwin, the bully.

"C'mon," said Elias, gesturing toward the starting line. "Let's see what an ex-cheechako can do in the 100-yard-dash." Will hesitated, but only for a heartbeat.

"I can beat you," Will said grinning widely. He fell in with the boys, paid his quarter and jostled for a position along the starting line.

"On your mark," shouted the starter. Edwin jammed himself into a too-small space at Will's left, elbowing a smaller boy aside.

"Get set!"

"No shoving, Edwin," Will said as he moved over to let the other boy back in the lineup.

"You're gonna lose, Cheechako. I don't care if you *are* supposed to be some kind of hero."

"Go!"

Edwin wasn't ready, and started badly. Will took off like a shot, pounding down the hundred-yard stretch, shoulder-to-shoulder with Elias. His feet felt wonderfully light in his new tennies, like he was running on springs. With each step, a puff of river silt, fine as flour, shot out behind. Then it was time to lunge with his chest for the tape, hitting it, breaking it simultaneously with his friend.

"We won!" shouted Elias, pounding him on the back. "Five dollars for each of us!"

"There's money? I didn't know there was money in it," Will exclaimed. Together they collected their prizes, then drifted back to the store to pay back Grandma Coghill's quarter. Will felt flush, so he bought each of them a Coke.

The afternoon passed slowly, easily. Sitting on the wooden bench in front of the store, watching the three-legged races, and the egg toss and listening to the firecrackers and the bottle rockets, Will felt an old feeling he hadn't felt for a long time.

"I feel at home," he said to Elias, "like I belong here."

"Lucky," said Elias. "Because this is your home." But then he sighed in exasperation.

Will turned his head to see what was bugging Elias. Edwin was pounding down the wooden sidewalk with his chubby fists clenched at his sides. Behind him trailed several guys, and Will could see they were trying to talk him out of whatever he had in his mind.

"Get up, chicken," he said, stopping directly in front of Will.

"Bad news," said Elias. "He's not chicken."

Will's stomach clenched up hard. From under the bench came a low growl.

Will jumped to his feet so abruptly that Edwin startled backward as though punched, and nearly fell. That made him look stupid, which made him act even more stupid.

Edwin took his position, bobbing and weaving, fists up. "It's me and you. Come on—unless you're a cheechako chicken." He thumped Will on the chest. "Cheechako..." Shove. "...chicken…" Thump.

It startled Will to realize that he'd grown taller than Edwin since they last faced-off. Will watched Edwin hopping and swaying. He looked quite comical, actually. Will suppressed a laugh. Elias grinned. Daniel and the other boys snickered.

"Come on Cheechako, or are you chicken," taunted Edwin, but the laughter took some of the wind out of his sails.

"Yeah, I'm chicken," said Will with a grin. The knot in his stomach released and the fear fell away.

He turned away from Edwin to the other boys.

"Anybody for a game of basketball?"

"Yeah, let's play B-ball," said Daniel.

Will turned back to Edwin. "What about it, Edwin? You up for a game?"

Edwin dropped his fists, dumbfounded. Not sure what had just happened, he shrugged. "I guess so."

As a pack, the boys raced off to the schoolyard, stopping to pump up Daniel's old Voit Allstar.

CHEECHAKO

Choosing teams, Daniel chose Elias who chose Will. Will thought, *What the heck!* and chose Edwin. Edwin, who still didn't have a clue, smiled gratefully and actually played pretty well, even with Blackie dodging and barking underfoot.

All night long they played basketball in the twilight of the midnight sun, only heading home at breakfast time, hungry and tired—and friends.

ABOUT THE AUTHOR

Jonathan Thomas Stratman is a writer, musician, and video producer who divides his time between Port Townsend, Washington and restoring an 1893 Victorian home near Eugene, Oregon. He is married to Billie Judy, also a video producer as well as a flower portraitist and copyeditor. He has known her since they were about Will's age.

Made in the USA
Middletown, DE
27 May 2017